NIGHT PICNIC

Literary Journal

VOLUME 7, ISSUE 1

FEBRUARY 2024

Night Picnic Press LLC
New York, New York

NIGHT PICNIC: Literary Journal   Volume 7, Issue 1 • February 2024

Igor V. Zaitsev, *Founder, Publisher, and Editor-in-Chief*
Gordon Stumpo, *Managing Editor and Art Director*
Oksana Williams, *Editor*

editor@nightpicnic.net
www.nightpicnic.net

Night Picnic is a literary journal founded in 2018. We publish novels, novellas, plays, short and flash stories, fairytales and fantasy for adults, poetry, interviews, essays (including popular science essays), letters to the editors, and artwork. We seek to share and celebrate all that is strange, dark, jubilant, complex, confusing, scary, mystical, fantastic, multidimensional, and metaphysical. Published triannually in February, June, and October by Night Picnic Press LLC. We are grateful for donations of any amount. They support the publication of the journal.

For single print copies ($15) and digital versions ($5), please go to www.amazon.com and the Kindle store. Subscriptions to Night Picnic Journal are $35 (3 issues), $45 for libraries. Foreign orders, please add $10. Subscriptions are only available by mail through Night Picnic Press LLC. Please send checks or money orders to:

Night Picnic Press LLC
P.O. Box 3819
New York, NY 10163-3819

© 2024 by Night Picnic Press LLC
© Logo design by Igor V. Zaitsev
© Cover design by Gordon Stumpo
© Cover photo by Igor V. Zaitsev
© Illustrations by Gordon Stumpo
Printed and bound in the USA

ISSN 2639-7625 (Paperback)   ISBN 978-1-970033-33-5 (Paperback)
ISSN 2639-7633 (eBook)   ISBN 978-1-970033-34-2 (eBook)

All rights reserved. No part of this periodical may be reproduced by any means, including but not limited to, graphic, electronic, or mechanical, including photocopying, recording, taping or by any information storage retrieval system without the written consent of Night Picnic Press LLC. The journal's name and logo and the various titles and headings herein are trademarks of Night Picnic Press LLC.

This is a work of fiction. Names, characters, places, and incidents are fictitious. Any resemblance to actual events, locales, or persons, living or dead, is entirely coincidental. The views expressed in the writing herein are solely those of their respective authors.

NIGHT PICNIC • Volume 7, Issue 1 • February 2024

CONTENTS

AUTHORS AND EDITORS

	page
Biographies	4
Past Contributing Authors	5

FICTION

The Perfect Structure .... Brandon Michael Cleverly Breen	7
The Second Life of Tommy Parker .... Laura Stone	13
Collecting Snow .... David Hinson	19
Yesterday .... Alice Baburek	27
Kiss of the Cailleach Bheur .... Nancy Pica Renken	31
The First House .... Megan Liscomb	37
Star Pupil .... Michael David Wadler	43

POETRY

From the Center of an X & other poems .... Glen Armstrong	75
Cardinals & other poem .... E.L. Douglas	78
The Go Rub Yourself Sonnets .... Jack Granath	81

AUTHORS AND EDITORS

Armstrong, Glen. Poet. Teacher. Author of *Night School: Selected Early Poems*. Pontiac, MI, USA.

Baburek, Alice. Writer. Avid reader. Animal lover. Retired from one of the largest library systems in Ohio. Published in Querencia Press: *Fall Anthology 2022* and *The Rabbit Hole: Weird Stories Volume Six* (2023). Brooklyn, OH, USA.

Breen, Brandon Michael Cleverly. Writer. Weight lifter. Boston native. PhD student of literature in Italy. Professor of Italian at Boston University Padua. Author of several short stories in Italian and English. Padua, Italy.

Douglas, E.L. Student. Pharmacy Tech. Poet. Winter Garden, FL, USA.

Granath, Jack. Librarian in Kansas. Poetry published in *Poetry East, New York Quarterly,* and *North American Review.* KS, USA.

Hinson, David. Editor. Writer. Published in *Greyrock Review*. Washington, DC, USA.

Liscomb, Megan. Writer. Lifestyle Editor. Doodler. Published in *Bravura* and *OK Whatever.* San Diego, CA, USA.

Renken, Nancy Pica. Writer of short stories and flash fiction. Published in *Wyldblood Magazine* and *Strangely Funny.* Denver, CO, USA.

Stone, Laura. Published short story writer. English and Journalism BA Honours graduate. Avid fan of Gothic literature. Bristol, England.

Stumpo, Gordon. Managing Editor & Art Director of *Night Picnic.* Published scholar, writer, and illustrator. Mentor. Educator. Fashion designer. New York, NY, USA.

Wadler, Michael David. Author of the book *Twenty Odd Pieces.* Theatre director, dramaturg, and playwright. Renaissance Speakers toastmaster. Glendale, CA, USA.

Williams, Oksana. Editor of *Night Picnic.* Bibliophile. Graduate of Irkutsk State Polytechnical University and math teacher of the American International School of Bucharest. Bucharest, Romania.

Zaitsev, Igor V. Founder, publisher, and editor-in-chief of *Night Picnic.* Biologist. Poet. Writer. Professor at Borough of Manhattan Community College, the City University of New York. New York, NY, USA.

PAST CONTRIBUTING AUTHORS

Gale Acuff • Edward Ahern • Penel Alden • Angelica Allain • Samuel J. Allen
David M. Alper • James Arthur • Douglas Balmain • Evan Baughfman • Ariel Berry
Mads Bohan • A. C. Bohleber • Francesca Della Bona • Katy Boyer • Charlie Brice
Tori Bryl • David Capps • Frank Carellini • Grant Carriker • Natalie K. Christiansen
Robert Ciesla • Emme Clause • Tim Connors • Kalynn Michelle Cotton
Mary Eliza Crane • Tanner Cremeans • Kaier Curtin • Alex Dako • Holly Day
John Delaney • Shane Delaney • Lenny DellaRocca • RC de Winter • Frank Diamond
Leslie Dianne • William Doreski • Joseph J. Dowling • Karen Downs-Barton
Gary Duehr • Michael Dubilet • Emily Dupuis • Tonya Eberhard • Alan Elyshevitz
Massimo Fantuzzi • E. W. Farnsworth • Uzma Fathima • Halley Fehner
Jonathan Ferrini • Fayette Fox • Cass Francis • Philip Gambone
Roberta Hartling Gates • Marshall Geck • TeaJae Glennon • Rich Glinnen
D. C. Gonk • Julian Grant • Gerri R. Gray • John Grey • Jordan M. Griffin
Christopher Hadin • Max Halper • Marcus Hansson • Spencer Harrington
Colton Heitzman-Breen • Bryan E. Helton • Laura E. Hoffman • Michael Paul Hogan
Jery Hollis • Brent Holmes • J.D. Hosemann • Thomas Hunt • Rollin Jewett
Briley D. Jones • Steve Karamitros • Mark Keane • Suzane Kelsey • Mark Kessinger
Harry Kidd • Steven Kish • Jacob Klein • Hunter C. Koch • Alyona Kondratyeva
Petro Kovaliv Jonathan Koven • Ryan Thomas LaBee • Andrew Lafleche
Lee Landey • Matthew Lane • Aaron Laughlin • Keon Lee • Jamie Leondaris
Todd Lewis • James M. Lindsay • Susie Little • Sara Long • Russ López
LindaAnn LoSchiavo • Paul Luikart • Simina Lungu • Kim Malinowski
Davey Maloney • Laura Manuelidis • Tim McHugh • William M. McIntosh
Eric McLaughlin • Laura McPherson • Hannah Melin • Skyler Melnick
Ivana Mestrovic • Jack Miller • Paul Mills • Thomas J. Misuraca • Zach Murphy
Kamran Muthleb • Paula Reed Nancarrow • Ben Nardolilli • Martina R. Newberry
Emily Newsome • Barbra Nightingale • Anna Novikova • Oleg Olizev • Josiah Olson
Vincent Oppedisano • Jaime Paniagua • Geena Papini • Rachel Anne Parsons
Kelly Pavelich • Elizabeth Paxson • Kristopher Pendleton • Simon Perchik
Barton Drew Perkins • W. C. Perry • Joseph Pete • Laura L. Petersen
Christina E. Petrides • Patrick Pfister • Thomas Piekarski • Amanda Postman
John Pula • Alan Rice • Richard Risemberg • Frank Rivera • Shannon Roberts
Joshua Robinson • Radoslav Rochallyi • Frank Roger • Brian Rosten
Claire Russell • Rachel Sandell • Kamil Sariyev • Mark Scharf
Noelle Shoemate • Steven Schutzman • Beatriz Seelaender • Margarita Serafimova
Evan James Sheldon • G. T. Shepherd • Kelli Simpson • Vladimir Slovesnyy
Paul Smith • Liza Sofia • Julia Solomakha • Carolyn Sperry • Alex Stearns
Michael Stein • J. J. Steinfeld • Travis Stephens • Emily Stevens • Gordon Stumpo
David Summerfield • Patrick ten Brink • Simon Tertychniy • Harrison Cody Thrift
Steven Thomas • Charles Townsend • Caryl Gobin Ulrich • Rebekah VanDyk
Robin Vigfusson • Eugene Voron • Tiffany Washington • Jason Wallace • Carla Ward
Kim Welliver • Phil Wexler • Jack Wildern • Sybil Wilen • Christopher Williams
Lucky Williams • Ryan Gary Williams • Erin Wilson • Cassondra Windwalker
Mariah Woodland • Ian Woollen • R.S. Wren • Ben Wrixon • Igor V. Zaitsev • Ann Zhang

Igor V. Zaitsev, photograph, 2022.

The Perfect Structure

Brandon Michael Cleverly Breen

"Class, there's someone very special I want you to meet." Twenty pairs of five-year-old eyes stared up at Ms. Robertson. "This is Michael and we're getting married this weekend." A wave of silent understanding passed through the group of kindergarteners.

"Congratulations!" shouted one voice that couldn't quite distinguish the difference between r's and w's yet. Murmurs of agreement chorused through the children.

"Do you love him?" demanded another voice.

Ms. Robertson giggled and looked Michael in the eyes. Michael chuckled back, captivated by her bright smile.

"I love him more than anything in the world. But, sadly, that means you'll have a substitute all next week."

Groans of protest went through the five-year-olds, but they knew this was important. They understood.

* * *

"You might feel a light tug, but the Novocain should take care of most of the pain," the dentist told his patient. She murmured her consent. "Ready? One, two, three... and it's done." He dropped the tooth onto a tray on the side table. His assistant began to clean off the patient and switch her seat into the upright position.

"Did you want your tooth, Sarah?" The dentist asked. "Or should I just dispose of the little devil?"

"You can just toss it," she said through a mouthful of gauze.

Perfect.

After the patient left and the assistant was helping someone else, the dentist made sure no one's gaze was on him as he stuffed the small, white ball of enamel into his pocket.

He was as giddy as a child when he got home from work that day. The excitement echoed through the house as he tiptoed down the rickety basement stairs and flicked on the blaring fluorescent lights. The room was illuminated in a blinding flash of white as hundreds of teeth shone like pearls under the artificial glare.

"Beautiful, so beautiful," the dentist murmured. He walked over to his display of molars to look for a spot to put his new prize. He wiped it off with a cloth and placed it on a small plastic stand. Then he took out a black Sharpie and carefully wrote on a label underneath: "Sarah, female age 32, October 2."

The dentist stepped back to admire the new addition to his collection. A low buzz sound emitted from the light bulbs. The dentist stood drenched in pure white light and smiled.

Every tooth had a story. Every tooth was like a dear friend to him. Every tooth was like a page in a diary that the dentist hoped he would never stop writing. He remembered the first time he ever lost a tooth. He was seven years old and he recalled the memory with a euphoric fondness. He had felt his loose tooth for a week and one day he was pulling on it in front of his bathroom mirror when it fell down into the sink with a squirt of blood. Even at such a young age he realized that that was the most beautiful and pure thing he had ever seen, stained by the blood of his mouth. He was ashamed that he had dirtied this purity and spent ten minutes washing it in the sink. He knew he would keep that tooth forever. The next morning his mother had asked him if he forgot to leave his tooth for the tooth fairy, but he just told her he was too old to believe in that stuff.

Walking over to his small collection of children's teeth, he looked at this tooth as he reminisced. It would have rotted years ago if not for the dentist's meticulous attention. No part of the tooth was probably organic anymore, but that didn't matter to him. As long as it retained its original beauty. The dentist shuddered as an erotic chill shook his body. He loved his collection of teeth. They were beautiful; they were pure. They understood him.

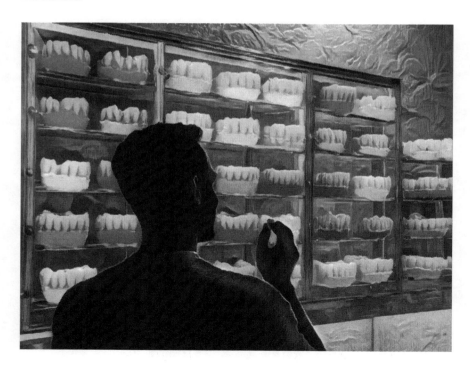

***

Ms. Robertson was at a Starbucks the day she met Michael. Thinking back on it, she laughed at the irony. Most people would consider that such a typical, cliché meeting, but the fact of the matter was Ms. Robertson never went to Starbucks. Hell, she didn't even like coffee. She had a long weekend. The police kept questioning her about the disappearance of her next-door neighbor, and she was developing a new program for the children. It was just a simple anatomy lesson about the bones in the human body, but explaining it to children was proving more difficult than she thought. Ms. Robertson stifled a yawn as she waited for her coffee. What she really needed was a shot of tequila.

"Tired, eh?" came a voice next to her.

Ms. Robertson tilted her head to get a view of the person who spoke. He was a middle-aged man with broad shoulders and dark brown eyes. He wasn't particularly attractive, but his cheekbones gave his face the perfect structure. Ms. Robertson flashed him a little smile as she registered his features, barely realizing that the barista was calling out her name.

Ms. Robertson shook her head a little and grabbed her coffee. She smiled again at that man as she went to leave.

"Excuse me," he called out, "I'm Michael. This might be crazy, but would you like to go out sometime?"

***

He remembered the day he decided to go to medical school to be a dentist. He was twenty-two at the time and had a meager collection of teeth that consisted of his own that had fallen out and others that he had stolen, either during elementary school when his classmates' teeth fell out, or during high school sporting events when rough tackles knocked out his teammates' teeth. But his craving — no his *need* — for new, beautiful teeth was becoming insatiable.

His roommate had perfect teeth. Never touched by the perverted metal of braces. Never stained by disgusting junk food. Never fouled by the gross hole of a cavity. In a straight line of pure whiteness. These teeth occupied his dreams. It became torture to sleep in the same room as his roommate knowing those teeth were behind his unconscious lips. Maybe, just maybe if he were only to touch them, he would be able to calm his desire. Maybe if he could just caress the smooth, pearly surfaces, then he could suppress the awful thoughts that had been occupying his mind.

Rip them out of his jaw! Smash his head in! Slit his throat! Get those teeth! Kill! Teeth! Perfect teeth! Kill! Kill him! KILL HIM!!!

"Stop!" He would yell to himself as he cradled his head in his palms. He didn't want to harm his roommate, but he needed to, at the very least, touch his teeth.

The dentist stared at his sleeping roommate from across the room. *What time was it?* He didn't know. He'd been kept awake by the beating of his heart and the knowledge that those teeth were here; they were here, and they could be his. He let out a low breath and decided to move slowly. He threw the blanket off his body and crawled over to his roommate's bed. He stared at the roommate's lips for a minute and his mouth began to water thinking about what lay behind them. *Just a touch. Nothing crazy, just a touch will satisfy me.*

Slowly, ever so slowly, the dentist moved his finger to his roommate's lips. He felt the dampness of saliva on his fingertip and pushed with a little more pressure, until the roommate's lips parted and suddenly his finger hit something hard. Teeth. They were so smooth, so perfect. The dentist couldn't help himself, he let out a low moan. The roommate's eyes flew open and he jerked his head back.

"What the hell are you doing?" he yelled.

"I..."

Threatened! Teeth! Get them! Before he gets you! They're yours! Need! Need them! Beautiful! Pure! Act now! Go! Now! NOW!!!

The dentist grabbed the roommate's head and bashed it against the wall. The roommate tried to retaliate, so the dentist slammed his head harder. And harder. Blood began to seep down the wall. Again. Blood stained the dentist's face. Blood stained the sheets. He kept slamming the head again and again until he couldn't recognize it anymore. Then he lay the still body down on the bed and opened its jaw. The teeth were still in perfect condition. He had exactly what he wanted. But what had he done? He had killed his roommate.

"I'm not a monster," he assured himself, "I'm a collector. Like of fine wine or comic books. This is an art. I did nothing wrong." He needed to feel strong and confident in his actions, otherwise he would lose his sanity if he kept second guessing himself.

The dentist then put himself to work and didn't stop well into the next day. He extracted every precious tooth and then had to get rid of the evidence. By the time he was finished his room was spotless, the roommate's body was gone — really gone, destroyed, never to be traced back to the dentist — and his pants were stained with bleach.

He felt something close to ecstasy. He had what he wanted, but it was a messy process. He needed some way he could still... collect. And not run the risk of being in trouble with the law. It hit him like divine inspiration: dental school.

* * *

As soon as the dentist saw her smile, he knew he needed to have those teeth. It was like someone had taken away his oxygen and he was struggling to breathe. He needed those teeth to survive, he was sure of it. He felt his tongue dampen with moisture and the zipper on his pants suddenly became tighter, more constricting. The perfect size, the perfect bright white. So pure. He would do anything he could to get those teeth. But he needed to be smart about it. He didn't want to have to resort to violence again. She was leaving, quick! He couldn't think, he was driven by an animalistic desire for those

teeth. *Obtain! Acquire! Need, neeeeed! Hunt! Go! Attack! DO SOMETHING!!!*
 His voice was coming out of his mouth before he could even register the words: "...cuse me, I'm Michael. This might be crazy, but would you like to go out sometime?"

* * *

Michael never expected to fall in love with Ms. Robertson, but he guessed the sensation he was experiencing now was pretty close to love. But the dentist never lost sight of his main goal. For two years he had been plotting, gaining her trust, earning her love, all for her teeth. He couldn't do any other collecting during this time, he was obsessed with her teeth and hers alone. Every time they kissed, he brushed his tongue softly against her teeth and it drove him crazy. Being able to feel them in a warm, live body was almost as good as having them for his collection. But only almost. Did he keep her intact and settle for them in her mouth just because he had grown to care for her? But no, he couldn't. That would be a weakness and he wouldn't have it. He'd been battling this weakness for two years, and now that he had been married for three weeks he needed to act now, before any more time passed. He needed those teeth for his collection.
 Michael was picking Ms. Robertson up from work this evening (she had kept her name at school so the children wouldn't get confused). They were supposed to go out to dinner. But the dentist would tell her that he had forgotten something at the office. They would go there and he would get her in one of his chairs... and then he would finally have his teeth.
 The sky was dark as he drove to the school and the raindrops fell on his windshield one at a time, until the sky opened up and a flash of lightning exploded and then he had to put his wipers on high speed so he could see the road. The ominous weather was quite appropriate. The dentist giggled.
 "Hey, honey," Ms. Robertson said as Michael walked into her classroom. She was bending over to pick up some Legos left on the ground in the play area. "I'm just cleaning a few more things up." Michael walked over and grabbed her from behind.
 "Take your time, sexy schoolteacher," he whispered in her ear.
 Ms. Robertson turned around to kiss him.
 "You're beautiful," she said to him, and then, after a moment, "I want you to know that's why."
 "Why what?" Michael laughed. "Why you love me?"
 Then, beyond his wife's face, he saw one of the kindergarteners emerge from behind a bookcase. He was holding a big toy dump truck.
 "Hey, little fella," Michael said. "Honey, did you know one of your kids was still in here?"
 Michael let go of his wife and looked at the kid. "Where are your parents, buddy?"
 The child smiled. Rain splashed against the classroom windows as he lifted the dump truck above his head and then brought it down on Michael's hip bone. The dentist let out a yell and fell to the floor.

"What the hell is wrong with this kid?" A flash of lightning illuminated the room more clearly and the dentist saw another child crawling out of the play area holding a Lego statue. Three little girls came out of the coat area holding umbrellas. The dentist whipped his head around as children appeared on all sides of him carrying toys, books, videotapes. Seven, eight, nine... he couldn't count but it looked as if Ms. Robertson's entire class was there. The child with the Lego statue was the first to approach the dentist. He threw the hunk of Legos at the dentist's face and the dentist cried out in pain. One of the umbrella-wielding girls jabbed the sharp tip into the dentist's eye. He screamed and began waving his arms frantically trying to bat off the children. One, two of them fell down, but they kept surging. Smashing toys onto his face, into his sides, onto his legs. The dentist couldn't feel his face, he could barely see, he couldn't find enough strength to lift himself off the ground. One child bit him in the stomach. Then another bit him on the nose. And then they had all abandoned their toys and were biting. Everywhere. Tearing at his skin with their underdeveloped teeth. Biting into his flesh as if it were candy. The dentist screamed and screamed until screaming and pain became the only thing he ever knew.

Ms. Robertson sat comfortably in her desk watching her children do her bidding. The flashes of lightning allowed her to get a better look at the bloody mass of rags and flesh and bone. Soon it would be over. The children were quick and efficient. They knew this was important. They understood.

Ms. Robertson stayed in her classroom late that night cleaning up. When she finished, she sat down and began to polish her newly-acquired skull with a damp cloth. It was perfect, the most amazing cheekbones. It would be an excellent addition to her collection.

The Second Life of Tommy Parker

Laura Stone

I was driving home from work when I first saw him, running for his life like a mad thing. My headlights picked up his frantic form, cutting a jagged path down the country road, weaving from side to side.

The sight of a lone man, fleeing as if being pursued, was an alarming sight indeed. Factor in that I knew very well that this particular man had died over three months ago, and you had one puzzling situation afoot.

Fortunately, I'm the curious sort, otherwise any one of those facts may have had me hitting the accelerator.

I recognized his hair first. That flowing mane of gold, rippling past broad shoulders, matted with dirt and leaves. I'd spent a lot of time staring at the back of that head in my school days. He was beautiful. He should have been lying in a coffin. No man is perfect, I guess.

Occasionally, Tommy threw a panicked glance backwards. I sincerely hoped nothing was chasing him.

I drove very slowly in a wide arc around him. His movements were erratic and the last thing I wanted was to send him back to the grave without any answers. Idling a few feet ahead of him, I slowed to a stop before rolling down my window. Freezing air rushed into my car.

Craning my neck outside, I peered back at the frenzied figure. I had enough sense to stay in the car for now at least. I've seen enough horror movies in my time, thank you very much.

"Tommy? Yoo-hoo, Tommy Parker! That really you?"

I don't know, what else would you say, in my situation? It probably wasn't a "yoo-hoo" kind of moment but I was panicking.

It wasn't particularly surprising when he barreled past me, staring straight ahead as if the devil were hot on his tail. My headlights painted a pitiful picture. A flash of a frightened face, the whites of his eyes showing. He was wearing a suit, a real nice one, apart from the dirt that coated it. I could hear the wheeze of his breath, was hit by the stench of sweat and earth. Blimey.

Swearing under my breath, I unclipped my seatbelt and unlocked the door.

It was fortunate I'd just finished a shift at the pub. I was wearing trainers, perfect for standing on my feet pouring pints for hours on end. Or running after potential zombies.

I jumped out of the car and tore off after him.

"Tom! Tommy! How the hell are you this fast?" I puffed. Dead for three months and fitter than me. I was fuming. "Stop making me run, you know I hate running!"

My appeal was in vain. He seemed to be making a more controlled effort to sprint away from me, weaving less. It was infuriating.

"Tommy, will you stop?! I want to help you, please!"

He stopped so abruptly, I almost crashed into his back.

I gasped for breath but kept my voice calm. "There now. Isn't that better?"

The look he gave me suggested he did not agree. Wide-eyed and practically snarling, he held his palms out as if to ward me off, clawing at the air. He was over six feet tall, stocky and muscular. I couldn't see any obvious signs of injury. The thought that I could be a danger to him was almost funny.

Plus he had that whole "dead man running" thing going on.

"You be polite or I'm getting straight back in that car and leaving your ass out here!" I snapped, using the same voice usually reserved for unruly patrons at the pub. It was normally quite effective, but Tommy just looked baffled.

I had no intention of leaving him alone in the cold. There was more dirt on his face and I'd just noticed the state of his hands, coated in grime and cut to pieces. He was even missing a fingernail or two.

"Jesus!" I breathed at the sight. He flinched, and I tried not to take it to heart. Every inch of his body was thrumming with tension, clearly seconds away from bolting.

I couldn't have that.

"I'm Bonnie, remember? We went to school together. Smithy the Spitter's year group? Called him that because of all the spit..." I trailed off, realizing I was only increasing his confusion. "Never mind."

"Y-y-you..." His voice was rusty. Tommy lowered his hands a fraction.

"Yes, me. Bonnie. You know me," I smiled encouragingly.

"Bonnie?" A spark of recognition. His eyes gleamed in the dark. I could almost recall their vivid shade of blue. Dreamy.

"That's right," I nodded as if I were talking to a child or a nervous animal. I sure hoped he wouldn't bite.

"What? Where am I?" He wrapped his arms around his body, looking exhausted. "I don't remember—" Suddenly, he doubled over in a coughing fit.

I reached out, intending to thump him on the back or something. He looked so pathetic. Even in his distracted state, he flinched away from me, still coughing, body shaking from the effort.

He hacked up something, spitting it onto the ground with a splat.

A smattering of dirt.

I felt my features twist with revulsion but made sure my disgust was well hidden when he looked up at me. Tommy wiped his mouth with the back of his hand, looking apologetic.

He groaned. "Oh God, I'm sorry. I don't know what's wrong with me."

I did. I wondered how to break it to him. Tact was never my strong point. Should I do it right here?

"What do you remember?" I asked, trying to disguise the eagerness in my voice.

He frowned in concentration and I fought down an inappropriate smile. It was the cute furrow between his eyebrows that I remembered so well, whenever he was asked a question in class. Tommy Parker was never the brightest boy in our year, but he was the prettiest. Plus, he was always so nice to me — unusual for such a popular kid.

"I remember nothing. Oh no..." he moaned, making a lunge for me. It took everything in me not to recoil or lash out. He was just upset, I reminded myself. It didn't stop me longing for the cricket bat in the back of my car, for a split second. A girl could never be too careful coming home alone at night.

He gripped my shoulders, trembling with desperation as he hauled me closer. "There was nothing! Just this deep, black emptiness... Where was I?"

His voice went high-pitched with panic, remaining nails digging into my flesh. The scent of mulch was choking me with his proximity.

I placed my hands firmly on his biceps to support him. His knees were buckling. He looked so wretched, the last of my reservations were scattered. This was no monster; he was a miracle. Just a frightened young man in need of help.

Instead, he found me.

"I think you were dead, Tommy," I said gently.

He wailed like a wounded animal. It wasn't denial. I saw that he understood instantly. Probably had to claw his way out his own grave, the poor chap.

His legs gave out. I wasn't strong enough to bear his weight. He dropped to his knees, pulling me down with him. As I crouched on the hard gravel, I could only watch as Tommy Parker began to cry.

"Noooooo..." He folded his arms across his chest, rocking back and forth. I held on tight.

"It's true. I went to your funeral."

"Don't—"

"Almost the entire town turned up. Imagine that!" I smiled. "Isn't that nice? To be so loved?"

"Please stop!" he begged, and so I did.

The harsh beams from my car highlighted his grief-stricken expression. I could see tears streaming freely down his cheeks. I pulled him closer and held him in my arms. He resisted at first and then relaxed, shuddering against me.

"I really missed you," I added shyly, but I could tell he wasn't listening. Sobs wracked his entire body and my heart went out to him.

It felt like fate, me being the one to find him. One of my earliest memories of him was when I fell over in the playground, scraping my knees and wailing fit to bust. Tommy pulled stupid faces to make me laugh and that was all it took. I fell in a whole other kind of way. I wished I could stem his tears just as easily.

Such kindness was one reason why I couldn't drive past him.

It was a scenario I may have imagined once or twice in my life, trailing my hands through Tommy's hair. Not quite like this, of course. I intended to soothe but his locks were too matted. Some strands came away in my hand, along with a dead leaf or two. I mentally shrugged.

It was probably impolite to ask whether he was hungering for tasty brains, but it didn't stop me wondering. Tall poplars stood sentry either side of the dirt road, casting strange shadows that danced over us. It reminded me of how very alone we were.

"There now..." I murmured as he gripped me tight. If someone had told me that one day Tommy Parker would cling to me as if his life depended on it... I tried not to laugh at the ridiculous thought.

What next? I knew I needed to take care of him. Obviously he couldn't just go strolling back into town. Of course not. What else did he remember, underneath all that trauma?

"What happened to me?" he gasped into my hair, arms locked around my middle, surprisingly strong. I felt a flicker of unease. He smelt bad but that was understandable. What if he was just playing on my sympathies, drawing me close before going full George A. Romero on me?

He felt me stiffen and withdrew, revealing the same Tommy I had always known. A little messier, a lot confused, still recognizably himself. Paranoia was a terrible thing.

We released each other but remained crouched, separated by mere inches. I considered his question. How much could he handle?

I chewed my lip before deciding that honesty was the best policy. "You were hit by a car. They haven't found the driver yet. I'm so sorry, Tommy." Best to get it all on the table.

His look of shock was one for the ages. It wasn't the nicest news to deliver either. I remembered the horror of his death breaking through town, the raw grief of knowing I would never see that sunshine smile again.

"You mean a hit and run?" His voice hitched with sobs. "They just left me?"

I squirmed, now acutely uncomfortable. "I guess so."

Every day, we had waited for the driver to be caught, justice for Tommy. It was a dark period of time I prefer not to dwell on. The days had turned into months and life had moved on. Somehow, I didn't think Tommy would appreciate that information.

"You guess so?" Something dark passed across his features and I shuffled back a little.

"Hey now... remember what I said about behaving?" I tried to sound steely, nearly breaking under the intensity of his stare. Fortunately, he broke first.

"I'm sorry," he scrubbed his hands over his face, smearing trails of dirt. It made the whites of his eyes practically glow. "I don't know what to say. I'm just so tired."

After the dirt-nap he'd just taken?

"That's okay," I replied instead.

He jolted to his feet, startling me terribly. "Oh my God, my poor parents!" he cried, before another thought hit him. "Amy! I have to get to Amy! She needs to know I'm alright."

It was like he'd poured cold water down my back. Amy, Amy, Amy... It always came back to Amy. She was his girlfriend, his fiancée, if I recalled correctly. They'd celebrated their engagement in my pub, then held his wake there too. She'd looked so beautiful, so tragic. The strange cycle of life.

Frantic, he began to pace. "I don't think that's a good idea," I gritted out, slowly pulling myself to my feet. I had a feeling Amy was the type of girl who would run screaming for the hills.

I was never good enough, was I? How many lone women would be willing to pull over in the dead of night — if you pardon the phrase — to help a strange man who had seemingly risen from the grave? Not many, I bet. Yet here I was, risking getting my brains eaten. And here he was, pining for his waif-like girlfriend. Typical.

No matter how many years I had yearned for him, all those times spent helping him scrape through school... Tommy Parker and Bonnie Preston. Would he have ever glanced my way if we hadn't been forced to sit alphabetically? It was doubtful.

I thought we had a connection. He was always so kind to me. There was no one who would go as far for him as I would. That's why when I saw him, tearing down the road, I wasn't afraid. I knew I was the only one who could help him.

"I could take you to town," I hedged. He was too keyed up to notice the flatness of my voice. "But I think it's a bad idea, given the circumstances."

He finally spared me a glance. I shivered in the cold night air. A fox screeched in the distant woods, making us both jump.

"What do you mean? They need to know I'm alive."

"Some people won't understand," I suggested delicately. I could see he wasn't listening, didn't want to hear it. He was the golden boy of the town. He didn't know how quickly people could turn, how cruel they could be.

"Amy isn't like that," he insisted, looking like a Labrador, dumb and bedraggled. I rolled my eyes.

"Trust me. You don't want people grabbing their pitchforks..."

He wasn't paying attention, going off on a tangent. "Maybe that's why I'm here. I was taken too young. Perhaps I'm meant to find out who did this to me!" He actually sounded excited by the prospect. That piqued my curiosity.

"What do you remember?" I prompted again.

"Nothing yet." The furrow between his brows was back, clearly giving it some real thought. "A bright light, pain, a voice..." he shuddered. "It's too soon to think about it. I don't like it."

"I don't blame you, you poor thing," I said, with the right amount of sympathy. He'd heard a voice?

He was practically bouncing on the balls of his feet, pretty spry for a dead guy. "Can you take me to Amy? Please, Bonnie? Please?"

He sounded like a child. I watched him for a long moment as he wiped away his tears, jutting his chin out defiantly.

"Of course," I sighed, coming to a decision. How could I deny him anything? "Wait here a sec. I'm just going to fetch a blanket." I gestured vaguely in his direction. "Because of the dirt."

He still wasn't listening, kept pacing. No wonder the grave couldn't contain him.

I went to the car, got what I needed, and then padded back over to him, feeling truly weary.

Tommy stood with his head tilted back, eyes closed, bathed in moonlight. He was almost too beautiful, skin glowing in an uncanny fashion. I was afraid of him. I wanted to take care of him.

"I can always count on you, Bonnie," he said so softly. The hairs at the nape of my neck stood on end. It was exactly what I'd always wanted to hear. He looked unearthly, strangely peaceful. Was it an illusion? His hands were balled into fists.

"I'm sorry, Tommy. Truly, I am."

He opened his eyes as I swung the bat into his head at full force.

One hit was all it took, kind of like last time. His skull cracked — I heard it, felt it. I may not have the strength of an engine but it worked just the same. I didn't have to hold his hand and wait for the life to leave his body, he was just gone. I wished I could have told him that he didn't die alone the first time — I'm not a monster. That it was an accident, a moment of madness, a crime of passion... I don't know.

I looked at his crumpled form and sighed deeply. It was going to be a long night. At least the grave was already open, waiting for his return.

Hopefully it would hold him this time.

Collecting Snow

David Hinson

Lila sees you slipping away and gently kisses your shoulder. This close to sleep, you weren't expecting any attention, and it worries you. Lila usually pulls you back from the brink of dreaming only when she wants to talk about something she thinks you'll deflect if you're fully alert.

She grabs your arm and pretends to have trouble pulling you onto your side to face her, even though she does CrossFit and could probably bench-press you. You see the pretending as an attempt to seem playful, to disarm you. She finds and holds your hand under the covers. "You never say anything while we're having sex."

Her tone transforms it into a question.

It's unlike her to be this indirect. You decide to take her words literally, as merely an observation that requires no response. You don't have a useful reply anyway. Your exhausted brain produces vague attempts to connect the past and the present. Like how when you were younger and no one wanted anything from you except friendship, you felt ashamed of your sexual desires. Or later, how things you asked for in bed were met with giggles, hesitation, or refusal. Or how you've always hated your body and aim for invisibility when it's exposed, and speaking will draw attention. So, shame and humiliation? But that's too general an answer, and there's nothing to be gained from saying that out loud.

Lila squeezes your hand to pull you from your thoughts. Or maybe to wake you up. You don't know how much time has passed as you tried to think of something to say, but Lila spares you by asking something else. "Are you afraid of me?"

And you say no, hoping your reply isn't rushed enough to make her think you mean the opposite.

Lila releases your hand and rolls onto her back. "Michelle says you are."

Michelle, Lila's former roommate, had been in town and the two of you had lunch with her last weekend.

You stare at Lila's profile. Above her nose and out the window, snow falls. You consider asking whether she believes Michelle, but you worry about sounding angry. You place your hand on Lila's stomach to be physically affectionate as words fail you. She lets you do this and even lays her hand on top of yours. You ask what she's thinking.

"Why are you afraid of me?"

You think you're in over your head in this relationship and wake up every day wondering if it's going to be the day she stops believing you're worthy of her time or affection or generosity or any of it. And that's another thing you don't want to say out loud.

Your issue is that you don't know why she loves you. You've lied, exaggerated, and omitted so much. You've pretended to like, know, do, and have more than you do and to be more than you are, and you don't know what she's latched onto.

It's the ways you most differ from her that you try to keep secret. Lila lives in a newly-fashionable neighborhood within walking distance of the restaurants and bars you hear about most often at work. You live in a neighborhood so far away from the city's main development efforts that you doubt it will ever gentrify. Lila has visited every continent except Antarctica, and you have only been to the seven states where you have family. Lila has five young cousins and can speak to anyone younger than her with ease. You felt flustered and intimidated when a coworker once brought her preschooler to the office for the week she couldn't arrange child care. Lila has many friends, and some days you wonder if you have any friends other than her and the married couple you live with.

You think Lila has more than you in every way, and you think she'll leave you because of that. You decided early on that she was more than what you felt you deserved, but you pressed on. In conversation, you said little and nodded a lot. You looked up synopses of the TV shows and movies she mentioned so you could say something if they came up again. You listened to the most popular tracks of every musician she named. You never turned down a restaurant she chose. You experimented in bed only until you discovered what worked for her.

You don't think twice about self-suppression. You want to be like the people you know who can reveal themselves and be loved all the more for it, but you've convinced yourself that the less you reveal, the more likely the relationship will last.

Lila's out of bed now. She pulls on underwear and a sweater, leaves the room, and shuts the door.

You can't bring yourself to follow her because you don't know what you'd say. Instead, you climb out of her bed, turn off the lamp, and sit with your legs crossed on the bench she has in front of the window. The bookcases on either side of you, both painted black, are invisible in your peripheral vision, and it's easy to convince yourself you're floating. The hotel across the street that was not quite deserving enough to become a protected historical site is gone. The last of the debris from the controlled demolition was being carted away the first time Lila invited you here. You visited the website listed on the construction fence and found artist renderings of luxury apartments sitting atop retail space. You imagine it will be a grocery store offering food you've never heard of or a gym offering classes beyond your financial means and physical ability. But for now, the lot is a hole in the ground collecting snow, and beyond it you can see a part of the city's downtown core — partially-lit skyscrapers whose upper reaches have disappeared into low-hanging clouds.

Within your view now, also, is the baseball stadium where you and Lila met this past summer. Benny and Charlotte, the couple from whom you rent an upper floor and attic in a house miles from here, gave you season tickets for two seats in a box next to the third-base dugout. You initially refused them because of how much you suspected they cost. But Benny said he won them in a contest put on by the radio station he listened to when he was working on the Ford Galaxie he was trying to restore. You took them and didn't feel bad about not going to games. None of your coworkers, still the only people you really know in the city, liked baseball, and you didn't want to go alone.

But Benny and Charlotte noticed. The stairs to your unit are in a tiny foyer in the back of the house between a door that leads to the backyard and a door that leads to Benny and Charlotte's space. "You live here," Benny called from beneath his Galaxie the first Saturday you crossed the back driveway to go out. "Use the front door."

It initially made you uncomfortable to pass through their unit. But later, it had become so routine that you forgot that Benny and Charlotte almost always knew whether you were home. Three weeks into the baseball season, Benny said, "I've watched every home game so far, and you've been upstairs every time."

"You're young," Charlotte added. "You can sit in the house when you're eighty like us."

And so you went.

The two seats Benny won were in the front row of the box on the side toward home plate. You took the seat at the end of the row to put an empty seat between you and three old men who didn't acknowledge you. They each wrote in identical large-print scoring guides and drank beers that you later noticed came every other inning without being asked for. As soon as you realized this, a woman behind you said, "Oh no no. We used to have seats on the first-base side, but we got these when, Frank? Like five or six years ago?" and you realized that your boxmates were all regulars. Or rather, those immediately around you were regulars, and you projected that onto the thirty-or-so other people in the box. And you felt ashamed of being alone in what you assumed was a crowd of pairs and groups. So when you left after the extra innings, you decided you wouldn't come back.

Your initial thought was to keep up appearances for Benny and Charlotte, but the first time you left the house pretending to go to a game, you struggled to decide where to go instead. You went to the movies to see the most recent superhero release even though everyone at the office, in rare consensus, said it wasn't any good. You were almost home before you thought to check the game highlights on your phone, and you were lucky to think of that. As soon as you stepped inside the house, Benny called from the living room, "You see that catch?"

And yes. Yes, you had.

You kept this up, alternating between movies and plays. The shame of being by yourself in a crowd was less intense in the dark, and the screen and the stage produced a self-forgetfulness the field did not.

July arrived and brought with it the birthdays of all seven of Benny and Charlotte's grandchildren. For years, Benny had wanted to buy them all jerseys as gifts and had been waiting for a season when each age everyone was turning corresponded to a number on a player's jersey. He was a former small-business owner and never bought anything online, so he gave you his credit card and a list of players and shirt sizes one afternoon on your way out.

And so you went again.

The lengthened days brought temperatures so high that even the stadium's considerate design couldn't keep the seats cool. The box was empty when you arrived with your bag of jerseys just before first pitch. The second inning brought a high foul ball to your side of the field, and when you turned to follow it, you saw that someone had joined you. She was in the third row on the opposite side, as far away as she could be in the box, and she was wearing one of the special-edition pink jerseys the team had sold the previous October. She was looking over her shoulder like you were, waiting for the ball to descend. You felt self-conscious and thought that maybe someone was watching you watch her and not the ball, so you turned back to the field before a victorious hand emerged and cheers went up.

Two innings later, a batter sent a fastball straight into the pitcher's chest.

Several times, you've asked Lila why, during the subsequent delay, she came down from the third row to join you. And she's never given you an answer. You settled on thinking that maybe she felt as sorry for you as you felt for yourself for sitting alone. She was by herself only because friends who were supposed to have met her there bailed at the last minute. Whatever it was, by the seventh-inning stretch, she'd given you her number and invited you to a friend's party. You thought she was only being nice, but you continued your conversation over text for the rest of the week, and twice she said, "I'll show you when I see you at the party on Saturday."

At the party, she showed you a video of her cousins in their matching M&M's costumes from the previous Halloween and showed you how she and her friend Christina looked like twins in a way photos couldn't capture because their smiles differed so much.

As the summer wore on, she showed you her favorite bar, her gym and workout routine, her apartment, her bedroom, and the way she liked to be held.

And she invited you to experience a version of living you had seen only from the outside. It's a world of people following through on plans, of living close enough to walk home from late-night-early-morning parties, of running into people you know on the street, of feeling like you're part of a group, and of feeling like someone would notice or care if you left the city suddenly and permanently.

It's a world you never thought would have you, and even though you feel out of place, you want to be part of it. You feel as though you've abandoned an old self that, though comfortable and familiar and safe, you're happy to be rid of.

But your ticket to this new world is Lila. Without her, this new sense of who you are and what you feel you might deserve falls apart. And you worry that you give her nothing comparable in return.

And that scares you.

* * *

You didn't notice Jackson was afraid of you until Michelle pointed it out last weekend when the three of you had lunch together. When Jackson went to the bar to get more beers for the table, Michelle said, "He defers to you a lot."

You hadn't noticed, so you just shrugged. It wasn't only Michelle's words but her tone that made you nervous. She'd used that tone once before, years ago. That time, the words had been, "He certainly seems interested in that Lorena girl," "he" being the medical student you'd been dating at the time. Michelle claimed you were in denial because you hadn't, even after several months, come down from the high of being wanted by someone so desired himself. Which may, in hindsight, have been true, but you've always thought of yourself as a person not easily deluded, and it bothered you that you'd fallen so in love with someone that you'd lost the ability to evaluate your own life clearly. Michelle's comment about Jackson's deference challenged your sense of self again. You didn't want to believe something else had slipped past you, and you certainly didn't want to hear it from Michelle.

She took your silence to mean you needed proof, so she gave you examples: Jackson said nothing when the three of you were trying to decide where to eat, he retrieved your shoes even though you were going to have to walk by them on the way out, and he offered to pay for your part of the meal during the mere five seconds between when you thought you'd lost your credit card and when you realized you'd slipped it in your wallet backwards and were looking right at it.

You shrugged again. "So I have an attentive boyfriend."

But Michelle had more. "Every time I've asked something both of you can answer, he looks at you and lets you answer."

"Not always."

"Or he looks at you first like he wants your permission to speak."

Jackson was back within earshot, so you didn't answer this. He put the three bottles in the center of the table, and when his first gesture, even before sitting, was to move your empty bottle toward the unused fourth spot at the table and to put one of the new bottles into the sweat ring left behind, you met his eye, smiled, said thank you, and immediately looked back at your plate to avoid Michelle.

Michelle saw this as you admitting defeat. She turned toward Jackson and said, "So tell me about…" and then you learned new things about him.

You can't imagine you hid your humiliation very well as Michelle, in minutes, extracted information you've had months to discover yourself. If you hadn't previously been a server, you would have knocked over your beer in her direction to make her stop. So you sat through it. You learned that Jackson had never been out of the country (when he didn't have anything to contribute to discussions about travel, you had assumed he just hadn't been to the places you'd been). You learned that he lived five miles from here (he'd previously said he had no problem coming to your place all the time because you lived closer to his job, but you'd never asked how much closer). And you learned that his brother and sister, like you, both worked in state government (you did at least know he had two siblings).

You looked out the window to tune them out and spare your feelings. A cyclist pedaled down the sidewalk, and it made you cringe.

Jackson doesn't remember the day you almost ran over him on your bike on your way to CrossFit. You shouldn't have been on the sidewalk anyway, but you acted as though you were in the right. You screamed at him with your front tire stopped on his shoe, not thinking about how easily he could have pushed you or fought you or at least overpowered your voice with his own. You watched his eyes change. First, the fear and surprise gave way to anger at what you assumed he thought was your recklessness. But you watched confusion settle in, and when you pedaled away after saying God-knows-what, the last thing you saw was a kind of submission, like whatever you'd said had made him believe the near-collision had in fact been his fault.

And after the rigors of your class, you forgot about it.

But the day after that, you saw him again at that same intersection. You were stopped on the white line in the street this time, looking to the right to watch the red countdown in the box on the pole, and there he was below it, same jacket, same pants, same shoes. Same headphones, too (you thought at least that would have changed). His head bopped to a beat in time with the ticking seconds. You stared, as though a movement as subtle as turning your head away would catch his eye. You breathed maybe twice as you waited for the white figure to turn into a red hand and for that hand to stop blinking. When it did, you took the largest rolling start you've ever taken before the light turned green. Your legs felt unsteady as you pedaled away as fast as you could.

You later learned that Jackson had no routine on that street, and it was complete chance that you saw him two days in a row. But after that second time, you didn't forget him. Every ride down that block, you looked out for him. You so closely associated the person with the street that you almost didn't believe it when you sat in the box at the stadium that day in July, looked over, and saw the same profile you saw on the street corner. The empty distance between the two of you didn't stretch far enough for you to feel comfortable. He sat in your line of sight toward the infield. If he turned in your direction, you couldn't look anywhere else and you couldn't hide. The knot in your stomach wouldn't go away, and you considered leaving. But you thought maybe this was some kind of opportunity, neutral ground where you could apologize and make amends so you could bike down the street in peace.

So you walked down the steps.

He turned toward you before you reached him, and you saw in his eyes that he didn't recognize you. And that was all you needed to know. You felt no obligation to tell him what you'd done to him and no guilt for feeling that way. You were simply relieved. But you had committed. You couldn't just take that information and walk back up the steps, so you asked if you could join him, and he let you.

After you and Jackson hugged Michelle goodbye, the two of you walked back to your place, passing through, for perhaps the hundredth time, the intersection significant to only one of you.

It has taken you nearly a week to gather the courage to ask Jackson whether Michelle was right about him. And now here you are, self-banished from your own bedroom without an answer, sitting on the floor with your back against the couch, watching snow fall and waiting. You wonder whether Jackson's keeping something from you the way you have from him, and what it might be if he is. What did any of this mean if it started with such a big secret on your end? And what about since then, with all that Jackson hadn't mentioned to you but was perfectly willing to tell Michelle (with direct prompting, but still)? And if fear was why he didn't volunteer information, why was he still with you?

You can ask him. Your bedroom door's open now, and he's at your side again. The floor is cold and his body's warm, and you straddle him and ask him to hold you. He plants kisses across your collarbone and then from the point of your V-neck to your uplifted chin. And then you pull at each other's waistbands. You search his eyes, but he closes them as you move back and forth in his lap. And as his breathing changes, he speaks. It's the same sentiments you've heard from others (he thinks you're beautiful, and he loves

David Hinson

you), but coming from him, they carry the weight of originality.

And at the end, he says something that sounds different, but it gets buried in your shoulder as he holds you tight and loses himself in you.

Later, as you lay with him in bed again, you ask, gently, what it was.

He's almost asleep and doesn't open his eyes. He mumbles his answer, but you understand.

"Please don't leave."

You kiss his shoulder again, not to pull him back but to comfort him. And as you watch him slip away, you whisper, "I'm right here."

Yesterday

Alice Baburek

The old, decrepit woman leaned close to the overgrown rose bush. She hesitated a moment before carefully cutting the long, prickly stems. Brown petals spewed everywhere on the ground. It was that time of year again. Summer turned into fall. Cutting back the huge thicket of thorns surely guaranteed an enormous amount of healthy buds next year. Or did it? For a second she wasn't sure. Is this what she did last year for such an abundant amount of beautiful red roses? She sighed then took a step back. Did it really matter? Her shoulders slumped. A brisk wind floated through and rustled the surrounding trees. She pulled at the tattered, faded sweater then glanced up at the cloudy, grey sky. A slight shiver ran down her curved spine. It was time to go in.

Ana Kaplan waddled slowly toward the house. Remains of weathered paint patterned the aged home. Splintered wooden steps creaked under her frail frame. She set the rusted clippers down on the sagging porch. All her joints moved with resistance. Her arthritic fingers ached. Ana tried to ease the deep-rooted pain and rubbed her swollen knuckles. Every single day became more like a chore. Tricking her forgetful mind into thinking there was indeed a purpose to get up and dressed each morning. How she prayed for her time to end — end the misery called life.

"Hello?" called a timid voice from behind. Ana doubted her ears. She reached for the worn, brass knob. The warped door moaned in protest. She pushed a little harder.

"Excuse me? Hello? Ma'am?" The stranger's voice persisted. "I don't mean to bother you, but my car broke down about a half a mile from here. I tried to use my cell phone but I can't get service in this area for some odd reason. Can you help me? May I use your landline to call a tow truck?" Ana turned to face the unexpected visitor.

Her light brown hair was a mess. Curves of younger years carved out her reddened cheeks. She seemed out of breath for one so full of life. Wearing a silver hooded jacket and jeans. Ana stared at the out-of-place woman. She seemed vaguely familiar. Or did she?

"Do... do I know you?" asked Ana. The unseasoned female smiled.

"I don't know... do you?" said the strange woman. Ana's wrinkled forehead crunched in confusion. Her mind had to be playing tricks again.

"May I use your landline, Mrs...?" Her voice was soft.

"Oh, I haven't been a misses for years. Ana... Ana Kaplan. And you are?" insisted Ana.

"Rachael." She hesitated a brief moment then continued. "I won't take much of your time, Ana, I just need to call a tow truck." A pearly white smile shined. Surprisingly, her intense blue eyes left Ana feeling at ease.

"Come on in, Rachael. Help yourself to the phone. But I have to warn you, sometimes it works and other times... well, the connection just goes bad," explained Ana. Rachael moved swiftly up onto the unsettled porch. Ana hobbled inside with Rachael close behind.

"Would you like a cup of hot tea, my dear?" The warmth from the glowing ambers radiated the kitchen. Suddenly, Ana stopped in her tracks. "Rachael... well, what a coincidence, my middle name is Rachael. In fact, when I was growing up I often went by my middle name because Ana, at the time, seemed so old fashioned." Rachael, once again, smiled at the aging lady. Ana stared hard at the young woman's face. Why did she seem so familiar? Ana's mind raced through dozens and dozens of faces trying desperately to make a match.

"I guess we have something in common," said Rachel. "May I?" She pointed to the rotary on the worn end table.

"Why yes, of course," said Ana. Slowly, she turned her back to the young woman inching her way to the antiquated stove. Ana carefully filled up the dented teapot with water. She then placed it on the burner. Meticulously, she struck a match and held it to the escaping gas. Instantly a bright flame shot upward. She blew out the burning match.

Rachael held the stained receiver up to her ear. She tapped lightly on the hook-switch. "Hello? Hello?" Gently, she set the receiver back on the hook. "Nothing... there's no dial tone. I'll try again in a few minutes... if you don't mind me staying a bit." Without an invitation, Rachael pulled out the rickety, wooden chair and sat down by the deteriorated table.

"I don't mind at all. I haven't had company in years. My husband, Edgar, passed on ten years ago." Ana uncovered the plate full of homemade chocolate chip cookies. She eagerly set them near Rachael. "Don't be shy, please try my secret recipe." Ana winked. Rachael's smile reached from ear to ear. Immediately, she snatched the homemade morsel and took a huge bite.

"Wow! This is delicious! I like to bake, too," exclaimed Rachael. Ana studied the woman. Her bright blue eyes, round curved face, tiny nose, and her light brown hair. Why did Rachael look so familiar? Maybe she saw Rachael in town when she went to pick up supplies or the bank where her measly savings sat collecting nothing but dust. Suddenly, the sound of a whistle shrieked from the stove.

"Oh, let me fetch you a hot cup of tea to go along with my cookies," said Ana. Carefully, Ana poured two cups of hot tea. "Milk or honey?" she asked. Rachael swallowed.

"Neither, Ana...I like my tea with nothing added." Ana stopped for a brief moment.

"So do I." Ana placed the filled cup in front of Rachael. Rachael sipped at the steamy brew. Ana sat down across from Rachael. By now her entire body throbbed with pain. Her hands began to shake.

"Are you alright, Ana?" Rachael stopped chewing. Ana tried desperately to steady herself.

"Yes, yes, my dear. Sometimes when I work a little too long in the garden, I get the shakes. It'll go away after a spell... it always does." Her puffy fingers curled. "There's no fun in growing old. It seems the body just gives up while the mind... well, it follows close behind. But sometimes I can remember years ago, exact times and places, yet if you asked me about yesterday or the day before I'd have to think on it. Oh, not that I'm saying I do anything special each day. Once a week, I have the neighbor a mile down give me a lift into town to shop for groceries. I'm alone and keep to myself. Putter around outside as much as my body can tolerate and during the evening hours rock in my rocking chair reading the bible. Praying to the heavens above for my time to end. Yet, each day I wake up to face the aggravation called life." Ana let out a huge sigh. Rachael remained silent.

"Forgive me, Rachael. I didn't mean to carry on like I did. You're young and pretty and have your whole life ahead of you. Why, when I was about your age—"

Rachael cut the old woman off in mid-stream, "You were helping on the farm feeding and caring for the livestock while your father worked the fields. Your mother died while delivering your brother, Fred. May he rest in peace, too," said Rachael. Ana's eyes flew open wide.

"How... how did you know? How could you know? Did I tell you?" Ana doubted her memory once again.

"No, Ana, you didn't tell me." Rachael stood up. "Do you have any photographs of yourself when you were young?" asked the strange woman. Ana slowly pointed to the top drawer of the cabinet. Rachael pulled out the tattered album. Carefully she opened it and turned the yellowed pages. Seconds later she pulled out a faded photo and placed it on the table. "Take a good look at this picture, Ana, who do you see?" asked Rachael. Ana peered down at the ageless face. It was her when she just turned twenty. But as her eyes cleared a bit more she realized the similarities between her and the mysterious visitor.

"You see it, don't you, Ana... go ahead and say it," persisted Rachael. "Except for the clothes, we could pass as twins or better yet, the same person." Ana's head shot up and locked eyes with Rachael. How could this be? She didn't have a twin sister. So who is this woman? How did she know about her life on the farm? And why did they look so much alike?

"I know, it's a bit confusing, isn't it? Unfortunately, the explanation is just as confusing, if not mind-boggling. You see, Anna, that's me in the photo," said Rachael in a low tone. Ana's mind jumbled with long forgotten memories of days gone by. This didn't make sense. Not one bit.

"How could this be a photograph of you, when I know it is of me when I was about your age?" asked the old woman. But before Rachael made an attempt to answer, a searing pain surged through Ana's chest. Instantly, she grabbed the table with her gnarled fingers and fell back against the hard chair. Her eyelids flittered then closed for the last time. Ana would no longer awake each day and pray for her time to end. Her cries of merciless suffering had been heard and finally come to rest. The angelic peacefulness and pure essence of her soul welcomed the complete aspiration of eternal tranquility.

Rachael closed the battered book of yesterdays. She placed it gently on the table, then turned and walked outside into the green, grassy field. Moments later, her mystical spirit vanished within the swirling breath of heavenly winds.

Kiss of the Cailleach Bheur

Nancy Pica Renken

He sat among the grey stones, haunted by the last words his father had spoken to him, "Do not disappoint me." He would have wept had it been possible.

Brr! How much longer will I feel this way? How much longer will I feel anything?

Darkness fell in the clearing, and the newly-fallen snow blanketed him. Peeking out through heavy clouds and dense branches, the moon, bright and full, conjured an image in Diarmaid's mind of his father, a round-faced, burly man.

Those twinkling, brown eyes! I can see him now, romping around the dirt floor by our hearth, with fingers bent, as the bow glided across the fiddle. And that fiddle — calling forth ancient melodies and filling our cottage with echoes of love and loss, telling legends of old. Oh, God, those legends!

His father, Fergus, whose good humor was well known, underwent a metamorphosis when an early frost blighted the family's crops. Another vision took hold... his father before the journey: Fergus faltering among the ruined crops, clutching the remains of a withered stalk, crumpling it to dust between his fingers. His core heaving. Unintelligible sounds escaping his throat...

The failed crops had left Fergus no recourse. The meager finances, now drained, had caused him to travel to a distant city to plead with less-than-compassionate creditors.

Diarmaid shuddered. He could almost feel his father's bear-hug embrace from that late-autumn morning his father left the Highlands to begin the long journey to negotiate a loan extension. Tears slid down the big man's face as father and son faced each other in the village before the departure. Fergus scratched his greying beard as he gave parting words to seventeen-year-old Diarmaid, his only son.

"Take care of your mother and Bonnie," he had said. "We may just have enough food to last into spring. God willing, winter will hold off until I return." Then, he paused. "Diarmaid, you have been neglecting your duties and coming home drunk. This behavior worries me greatly."

Diarmaid had looked up at his father, wide-eyed.

Fergus frowned. "I know that Bonnie did the milking for you. She even chopped the firewood, didn't she?"

Diarmaid opened his mouth and turned his hands outward.

"No, your sister did not tell on you. I saw her taking on your chores when you were away with your friends or flirting in town with the lasses. I find your lack of responsibility disturbing."

"I would not—"

His father shook his head. "You have a wild streak about you. You're young. God knows I'd have a drink in the tavern on occasion with my friends when I was a lad, but I always got my work done. I worry about you and the man that you're becoming. I've told you the stories about what happens to those of poor character. They may be quaint, but stories have a way of taking on a life of their own. Alas, misfortune has struck. The last thing I want to do is to leave your mother, you, and Bonnie. I've worked hard and paid my taxes. I hope the bank considers that. I don't know what I'll do if they don't. But, in my absence, I need to know that I can rely on you. I need you to take on the responsibilities of a man."

Diarmaid's eyes examined the ground before him. "Yes, Father."

His father had sighed. "Be sure to set and check the traps. You'll need fresh meat. Can you do that?"

"Yes, Father," Diarmaid mumbled.

Diarmaid had been listening halfheartedly to his father's instructions until he caught sight of her near the holly tree, and then he stopped listening completely. The maiden had lengthy, blonde hair and eyes so blue they could hold a man's destiny or a whole world hostage within them. She smiled at the wayward youth, and a dimple appeared on her right cheek. Her gown was a swirling green that made Diarmaid think of seafoam. He knew she was not from the village. No village lass looked like her.

If only I could meet her, my life would be complete!

His eyes lingered on her beautiful face.

"Diarmaid! Did you hear anything I just said?"

"Of course, Father."

His father shook his head. "I hope so, son. Work hard. Take care of our family. Please follow my instructions and make me proud." Fergus looked into Diarmaid's eyes. "Don't disappoint me."

Diarmaid wished his father farewell. When he looked back, hoping to see the maiden, only a doe with bright eyes stared back at him next to the holly tree.

The doe's eyes almost look like hers. Diarmaid sighed. *If Father hadn't blabbered on so much, she wouldn't have slipped by me. No telling where she might be now. 'Do your chores.' Pish! And now, I've missed my chance to meet this maid.*

Diarmaid shrugged his shoulders, took one last look around town, and started for home. He had only walked a short distance when two of his friends called out to him, inviting him to join them at the tavern.

"Come on, Diarmaid. Why not tarry with us?"

Diarmaid smiled. *I'm not in any particular hurry to get home. The chores will be there. They always are. I might as well have a drink — or two.*

He followed his friends into the tavern. "Say, have either of you seen this bonnie maiden in a green dress? Long hair. Blue eyes. She was standing by the holly tree, but my father was lecturing, and I lost her.

They both laughed, having seen no such woman.

Inside the tavern, he had tried again. "Has anyone seen the maiden with blue eyes and long, golden hair? She was wearing a green dress."

The grey-bearded blacksmith laughed heartily. "I should like to see such a lassie, myself! I've heard no mention of this maiden. Is she real? Did you perhaps have a bit too much ale? Or might you be chasing after the *Cailleach Bheur*?" He chuckled again, raising his mug, toasting Diarmaid.

Diarmaid had rolled his eyes as he had taken a seat between his friends. The blacksmith's taunt angered Diarmaid. But, unbidden, memories of Highland tales curled before him like smoke rising from his father's pipe. Closing his eyes, Diarmaid could feel the warmth of those crackling fires mesmerizing him as lapping flames greedily devoured the split logs. Shadows had accentuated the face of his father as he had recounted the timeless legends of heroes, dark fairies, and howling banshees. Legends were never just stories to his father. Fergus would cross himself when speaking of malignant fairies.

Diarmaid had recalled his father saying, "Always be on your guard. A spunkie may befriend you on your path late at night, taking the form of a beautiful woman, gaining your trust, and then lead you over a cliff to your death. When you bathe in a lake, be mindful of your surroundings, checking there are no kelpies nearby.

"Winter is worst of all. She is a crafty crone, who can take the form of one much younger, bewitching a man with charms, leading him to his destruction. The Cailleach Bheur seeks out men of low character! Be forthright. Be upstanding and take responsibility. Choose wisely and do not be caught off guard. You would do well to heed my warnings."

The bonnie lass was not a dark fairy. Most surely not! Perhaps she is the niece of Mr. Forsythe, the richest man in town. That may well explain such a fancy gown. I will ask around.

He glanced over at the grinning blacksmith whose cheeks were rosy with ale. Diarmaid shrugged, dismissing any further negative thoughts as he drank steadily. Soon, his cheeks took on the same healthy glow.

* * *

In the long days following his father's absence, Diarmaid detested his chores. Finding idle excuses, Diarmaid absconded into the village as the firewood dwindled, the cows bellowed, and the stored meat disappeared. Diarmaid barely heard the protestations uttered by his mother. He could not shake the memory of the beautiful lass, ever hopeful that he would find her again. Nevertheless, no such maiden appeared. Diarmaid found that Mr. Forsythe had a wealthy nephew but no niece. No one else he knew had any knowledge of the mysterious woman.

One morning when the temperatures dropped, and the skies became a heavy grey, pregnant with snow, Diarmaid went to check the traps — that Bonnie had set the night before — near the forest entrance. His eagerness to check the traps resulted from his mother's directive, "Complete your chores, or you will no longer have a roof over your head! What would your father think if he could see you now?"

Father is not here. And clearly, neither of you have ever been in love. Love is more important than pointless chores. We have never starved, nor are we likely to in the future. Things around here never change that much.

To his delight, Diarmaid found a deer in the first trap. Its leg bloodied as it tried to free itself. Panting and struggling, its wide doe-eyes seemed to plead with him. Diarmaid laughed.

"Plead all you want, but it will do you no good. You are dinner. You might as well quit your struggling. I will not let you go."

Mother will be pleased. Fresh venison should cure her nagging. And father does not need to know that Bonnie was the one who set the trap.

Looking away, he raised his knife.

"Stop!"

His hand shook, and he nearly dropped the knife. A hasty glance confirmed that he was alone.

No one? I did not imagine that.

He turned back to the doe, and, to his amazement, there was the beautiful maiden crouched over the shaking animal. Freeing the deer. Wearing the same green gown as when he first saw her.

Diarmaid froze. His mouth hung open.

"Do not hurt one of *my* little ones."

Her voice, soothing as a mountain stream, held an undertone. Diarmaid blinked, dismissing it. He knelt there, staring, enthralled by her beauty. A breeze tousled her blonde hair. In a foreign tongue, she soothed the deer, bandaging its injured leg. Any concern for the family dinner completely evaporated. Nothing else existed for him at that moment. Gentle birdsong surrounded them. Warmth flooded through his core and flushed his cheeks. Feeling as though he could burst into song, he smiled. "My Lady," his voice cracked. "What is your name?"

The strange woman released the doe, and it skittered off into the forest. She smiled at Diarmaid and merely said, "Come with me."

Without hesitation, Diarmaid stood, dropping his knife.

Silently, taking his hand, the maiden led him into the darkening forest even though it was only morning. Great storm clouds swirled overhead, but Diarmaid did not notice.

She is real! They doubted me, but I knew she would return. My destiny is bound to hers.

As she held his hand, and they meandered along the narrow, wooded path, his heart raced ahead. The pair dodged branches in the increasingly-darkening forest. They passed a young male deer who had stopped to watch the youthful couple. Their path led them by the crumbled remains of an ancient altar, and, finally, the pathway opened into a clearing with large, grey stones positioned in a circular arrangement.

Dazed, Diarmaid looked around. *Where is this place?*

Discordant whispers filled the air, but he paid no heed.

The maiden paused, gesturing to the stones. Rumbling filled the air. A flock of birds cried out, launching from overhead tree branches. "They await me, my lovelies." Her large doe-eyes twinkled.

Inches separated them as Diarmaid leaned in. Incoherent whispers surrounded the young people, vibrating through them. Diarmaid, lost in the blue depths of her eyes, placed his hand about her narrow waist.

Her smile is my sunshine.

Diarmaid banished any niggling doubt. The blue depths of her eyes promised him everything. Nothing else mattered.

They kissed.

Her touch was the dew to parched blades of grass, unleashing a longing and desire that he had never known. He closed his eyes.

What strange magic is this? How can this be that I should find myself in enchanted woods, standing before mystical ruins, kissing the woman I have sought for so long? Fortune must have smiled down upon me. All this time spent searching for her, and she finds me! Yet, everything has been worth it. Everything. For this one moment.

Clamorous whispers surrounding them roared into flustered cacophony.

It is nothing, the chattering of squirrels or some other forest fauna.

The kiss, warm and moist on his lips, he would never forget.

Soft lips turned rigid, cracked, frozen.

His eyes flew open.

A savage wind swooped down from the north like an angry hawk, assailing Diarmaid with undue ferocity. He shuddered as the blast ripped through him, and a shroud of darkness descended upon the clearing.

His scream echoed off the grey stones, and Diarmaid trembled. Sweat poured down his forehead. All joy evaporated, along with the glamour.

A raspy cackle exploded through the clearing.

A blue-faced, larger-than-life crone leered above him.

No! No, it cannot be the truth!

Eyes bulging, he fell backward, clawing at the path, and crouched before the fiend.

The *Cailleach Bheur* loomed over him. The seafoam gown stretched into a deadly blue, gleaming of ice and malice. Wind poured forth from her mouth, chilling Diarmaid to the bone. The monstrous woman before him had haunted the fireside legends his father told. Flailing, as his limbs numbed, a whimper escaped him.

The Cailleach Bheur, eyes glazed, peered down her long, pointed nose at Diarmaid. She poked a withered, bony finger into his chest.

Diarmaid shook. "What have you done to me? I cannot move my arms or legs!"

"You did not heed your father, my lovely. Oh, yes, I watched you even as you sought me. I saw the chores you neglected to do. I saw the sister burdened by your neglect. I saw the despairing mother. I saw the heartbroken father — you chose me. You are mine, my lovely." Her cackle reverberated among the grey stones.

The Cailleach Bheur lifted a staff, fashioned from ice with a diamond handle, into the air. Striking the rod down before her, the earth quaked, the ground froze.

Diarmaid hunched, shielding his ears, as the crone bellowed into the midnight wood. Chanting, high-pitched invocations swirled into the vortex of the heavens, and crackles of lightning whipped up the gathering gale into cyclonic ferocity. He doubled over, retching into the clearing.

Am-am I shrinking? Diarmaid whimpered, huddling, a wounded child. Violent spasms coursed through his body.

The Cailleach Bheur swept past where he crouched between two stones. Deranged laughter echoed through the pitch-black forest. She lengthened in impossible stature, towering high above him — a giantess crone, cloaked in the cruel majesty of winter.

As he watched, the blue jaw unhinged into a gaping cavern, ushering out a violent fury. The Cailleach Bheur became the storm, no longer maiden or crone. Winter had come.

The ice demon howled throughout the night, lashing Diarmaid.

Why am I unable to move? What has she done to me? Help me! His lips would no longer move. The rumblings of the stones surrounding him amplified, pulsing through him. *I know I did not take responsibility. I disappointed my father. I am sorry. Please let me go.*

The fury continued.

***

With the coming of dawn, winter's fury dissipated. A fickle lover, she moved on, though her arctic chill and snowdrifts remained. Diarmaid, still immobilized, had survived the storm. The sun rose, casting shadows throughout the clearing, and his shadow fell before him. A horrifying clarity filled him.

I am not just among the grey stones — I am now one of them. Oh, God! What has she done? What have I done?

The First House

Megan Liscomb

We saw two houses that Saturday. The first sold while we were eyeing the turquoise tiles in the bathroom. Then the second one — the real estate agent called it "a fixer-upper" — sold while we were on our way there from the first. James, handsome and still tan from vacation, sighed in exasperation. He's always hated to lose. "This place is a 1970s nightmare," he said, squinting in disbelief in the driveway with his hands on his hips. "It's a dump!"

"It's a competitive market," the real estate agent replied with a smile and a knowing look.

I loved those tiles though, each one a slightly different hue. All together they sparkled like the underside of a wave. "When we find our house," I said on the drive back to our apartment, "we should do the bathroom just like that." He didn't answer, but I think he probably just couldn't hear me over the wind rushing in the windows and the radio and the L.A. sun and the L.A. traffic and the engine humming as he steered us along.

***

James read an article about the best day to look at homes, something about when the listings go up, so the next week we didn't wait for the weekend. He's so much better than me about knowing the best way to do things. So we went out on Thursday afternoon, which his boss didn't mind, but mine did. "If you keep skipping out on work like this, we might start questioning your dedication," he said in a tone that told me he already had doubts.

But it was okay, really. We saw three houses that day and put in our first offer for a two-bedroom that the real estate agent kept saying had "good bones." I still don't know what that means, but I think we could have been happy in that house, or the first house, or any of them really. Happy with those hardwood floors and stainless-steel appliances, sweeping dead leaves off the patio and watering the lawn. But we'll never know. The seller chose someone else.

***

"What you oughta do," James' father said from his seat at the head of his table, "next time, you should write the seller a letter. Tell them about yourselves. A nice young couple like you. If I was in the market, I'd love to sell you two a house." He swirled his glass of cabernet like a medieval lord.

His mother nodded eagerly at the other end of the table. We were all his subjects.

After dinner, the men went into his father's study while we women cleared the table, scraped the plates, rinsed each one, packed leftovers away, scrubbed the pans, hand-washed the wine glasses, wiped down the counters, loaded the dishwasher, and swept the crumbs off the floor. My new engagement ring, slipped off so I wouldn't lose it down the drain, bounced heavily in my pocket.

"I'm so excited for you two," his mother said, wringing dirty water out of a faded yellow sponge. "So many years ahead of you."

But that night I dreamed we were in the first house from the first Saturday, only it wasn't quite the same. The hallways were longer, impossibly long. And I was sweeping up decades of dust and debris into an enormous mound, pushing it along with me from room to room. As I worked, something made scratchy breathy sounds inside the walls.

I woke up sneezing. The room was dark and James snored raspily. I laid there for hours, staring up at the ceiling and taking slow, stuffy breaths through one side of my nose.

* * *

The next Thursday, James had a new real estate agent show us two houses on my lunch break. I don't really remember them though — I kept having to answer texts from work. He saw two more without me when my break was over, which I agreed to. He's just so much more particular.

We looked at all the listings together that night, curled up around his laptop in bed. They looked like they'd all been made in the same factory — white paint, subway tiles, gray cabinets and counters. I honestly couldn't tell them apart. "I think this new agent really gets it," James said. "We should put an offer in on this one." He tapped the screen, leaving a faint, greasy fingerprint behind.

"Okay," I yawned.

And then we were in the backyard at the first house again, digging up soil for a garden. We scraped the black earth with our spades and found stick after stick of fine white chalk stacked atop each other in the earth like lost catacombs. James used one to write his surname on the fence, the name I was dying to take. The rest turned into a pile of bones, small and frail like birds'. When I checked my phone in the morning for new emails and fresh bad news, a search was already open: "white chalk buried in yard meaning? spell??"

* * *

James had a letter all ready to go, detailing the life we hoped to build together in our new home, the good schools and the country club. He showed it to me while I sipped my coffee. "You know I'm still not sure about kids, right?"

"I know, crazy. I just wrote that 'cuz it's what you're supposed to say."

"All this stuff about me staying home—"

"It's bullshit, Emma, okay? You're overreacting again." I know I can be a bit oversensitive, but sometimes I wish he wouldn't remind me of it.

We argued until we had to leave for work, but he came home that night with good news: the offer was accepted. He hadn't changed a word of the letter. He brought home my favorite takeout to celebrate, cartons arranged on the coffee table like a buffet and a single red rose in a glass tube from the gas station.

***

"Make sure you do all the inspections," his father said, reclined in an Adirondack, surveying the view from the porch of his vacation home in Montecito. "I know it's the thing now, skipping things, rushing in, but you've got to keep your head. A home is an investment, never forget it!"

"And don't worry if it falls through, that's what the inspection is for," his mother said.

James smiled, showing his sharp white teeth. "I know, Mother."

"These things take time!" She chirped. "But you know something, I won't be able to relax until you two are settled in a nice place to start a family."

Then it was time to make dinner. His mother and I shucked corn, peeled potatoes and boiled them, snapped green beans, dunked four screeching lobsters in a pot, mashed potatoes, melted butter, squeezed lemons, ushered pans in and out of the stove, chopped a salad, sweated in our linen shirts, and drank white wine over ice. James and his father sat and talked in the shade.

***

That night, in the dark of the guestroom, I rolled over in bed. "What do you and your dad talk about all the time?"

James set his phone on his chest so that the light cast long shadows on his face like a kid telling scary stories at camp. "What do you mean?"

"Well," I took a deep breath. "I mean, your mom is great, of course, and you know that I love her, but it's just kinda weird how we're supposed to be relaxing up here this weekend and I've spent half my time doing chores."

"So you think she should do them all by herself?"

"No, no, I wouldn't—"

"So what, they give us a down payment with no strings attached and you can't even do a few simple things—"

"That's not what I said! It's just kinda weird, right? This whole, like, 'men in one room, women in the other' vibe. It's just, we're not gonna be like that, are we?"

He laughed. "We're gonna be like us, crazy." He kissed me on the forehead and mussed my hair like a little kid. I nestled closer to him, my ear pressed against his chest, and let the sound and rhythm of his breath rock me into rest.

Meanwhile in the first house, there was a baby waiting for me — the first realtor placed the cold and clammy thing in my arms when she handed James the keys. It had his nose with deep black eyes, chalky skin, and long, bony fingers. I put it down on the front lawn and it crawled around into the backyard, scratching at the earth with its small hands. The scratching in the walls was so loud we could hear it outside, even with the doors closed.

That morning I noticed dry, cakey dirt under my fingernails that I had to scrub and scrub to wash away.

* * *

The home inspectors found a whole laundry list of problems: termite damage, cracks in the foundation, aluminum wiring, and ancient plumbing. "It's a fucking shithole," James fumed.

He rescinded the offer and hired a new real estate agent. I wanted a break from all of it, but he couldn't stop. He tried to show me the listings but I didn't want to see them anymore. He spent hours on his laptop, on his phone. It made my stomach hurt, even though I knew he was only doing it to make me happy, to make us happy.

Sometimes, and especially while I was at work, I began having this strange sensation like I was floating just outside of my body, watching my hands move and my mouth speak like I was another person. It was amazing what my body could do without me. I started taking long walks again like my old therapist had recommended. I tried to reach her for an appointment, but she was all booked up for months.

"He's so ambitious!" His mother cooed into the phone as I strolled past a Spanish-style bungalow. She'd taken to calling me a few times a week just to chat ever since we got engaged. She said she'd always wanted a daughter, and now she had me. But I couldn't shake the feeling that I wasn't really the girl she had hoped for and she was just too polite to say so. "He won't stop until he gets what he wants, he's always been like this. You really are a lucky girl."

I had a coughing fit. Allergies.

"Are you alright dear?"

"Fine, fine, thanks."

"Well I'll let you get going. Give my love to sweet James."

Sometimes when I went out walking, I slipped my ring off in my pocket. James had insisted on a great big diamond even though he knows I don't like flashy things. I would run my fingertips over its points, feeling all the hidden edges. He just wanted me to have the best of everything.

* * *

The longer we were in the market, the worse things got. The prices kept going up and up and up, every week a new record high, and James asked his father for more money. I could never ask my family. When he got the money, we went on a date to celebrate. "Here's to you," James said, pouring champagne into my glass.

I felt outside myself again. We clinked glasses over a candle. The room buzzed with soft music and other couples' conversations. "Do you ever think about the first house we saw together?" I asked and watched myself bring my glass to my lips.

"The one we put in an offer on?"

"No, no, the first house, with the tiles that I liked—"

"That house sold months ago, baby girl. What are you talking about?"

"I don't know," my body said. "I just think about it sometimes."

He leaned in and wrapped one of my body's hands in both of his. "Hey, don't worry little one. I'm gonna find us a place really soon. Mark my words." And even though that was what I had always wanted — a husband, a home — I didn't feel reassured.

That night in the first house, I paced the halls listening to the scratching, scraping sounds inside the walls. It sounded like there was another family in there, trapped behind the plaster, struggling to get out. I ran my fingers over the walls as if they were printed with braille and I could read their secrets with my touch. In the morning, my feet ached like I'd been walking all night.

* * *

Two Thursdays later James texted me at work: "Put an offer in on this one," he said with a kissing face emoji and a link to a listing. "I have a really good feeling!"

The rest of the day went by in a gray blur. I kept opening spreadsheets and documents, clicking from tab to tab on my screen, just trying to look busy. Received an email from my boss: "The team is very concerned about the careless errors you've been making. If you want to stay here, you need to step it up." A coworker invited me for a coffee and I declined. "I'm just so

slammed," I lied with a smile. I watched my body leave at ten to five without saying goodbye to a soul. She just left and started walking.

I didn't know where she was going at first, but as we got closer, I could hear the scratching in the walls, the whispers, and the faint hum of energy rushing through the circuits of the first house. Following the sound, I got there before my body did. This time I was alone; no body, no James, no baby, no real estate agent. Just me and the dust, the black earth and bones, and the scraping, scratching, scuttling within the walls. All mine and mine alone.

I don't know how long it was that I was alone there listening. With my ear to the wall I could almost make out words, "Oooouuuuurrrrsssssssss. Nnnnnnoooooootttttt yyyoooouuurrrrsssssss."

But they were wrong, I knew it. "Mine," I whispered back, "all mine."

I see my body standing in the driveway. She doesn't know what I know yet. There is another family there, inside the walls, and it's up to us to cast them out. And then I am inside of her, moving her limbs like a marionette. The family in the walls, they don't want us here. But I have a plan.

We get down low and crawl into the backyard. "Dig up their bones," I tell her, "that'll teach them." So we dig, using her weak little hands, we claw at the hard earth. A baby cries. We dig faster. Her nails tear. "Good," I hiss, "that means it's working."

"Hey, what are you doing in my yard?" Someone says.

We don't look up. We dig deeper. A light flashes in our eyes and we squint. I want to screech like an animal, to puff up our body to scare them away from us. To piss in the hole so they can smell us. To scream that this place is mine.

"I'm calling the police."

We don't look up. We don't answer. We should have found the chalk by now. Something is wrong. We keep on digging, our hands frantic. We don't know what else to do. When the flashing lights arrive, we're still searching for it and our fingertips have just begun to bleed.

Star Pupil

Michael David Wadler

Prologue

Jesse Goodrich was far-and-away the brightest star in our high school firmament. And then, after graduating college, he suddenly blinked out, like some Unidentified Flying Objects have been known to do (more about UFOs later, much more).

At our ten-year reunion, many of us wondered what had happened to Jesse. None of us knew of his whereabouts. A few enterprising classmates, including me, had attempted to contact him by mail, but the letters were returned as undeliverable. Others searched high and low for him, but all hit dead ends. Speculation ran amok: he was a secret agent in Russia; he became an international jewel thief; he got lost searching along the Orinoco for El Dorado, the legendary Gilded Man (that was my guess, based on a Donald Duck comic book I had once read).

Curiosity morphed into mystery. Where in Creation was Jesse Goodrich? The truth, it turned out, was something so strange that none of us could possibly have imagined it.

I. High School

Jesse Ulysses Goodrich: brilliant — even a genius! Out of undisguised jealousy, most of us in high school referred to him as "*God*rich," but not I. That was way too obvious, as well as disrespectful. Instead, I made use of his initials "J.U.G." and referred to him as "Jughead." There was a slight resemblance between Jesse and the comic book character, mostly around the ears, so the name stuck. In retaliation, Jesse started calling me "Fat-Ass." For some reason (I can't imagine why!), that name also stuck.

Despite the name-calling, we were friendly competitors — but only in English class. That was the one place where I was remotely in his league. He knew more history than our history teachers, more Latin than our Latin teachers, and more chemistry than our chemistry teachers. But English, if taught correctly, is not a memorization subject; it's a creative subject. And creativity is the great equalizer.

I'll never forget our Great Debate. One day, I happened to mention that I believed in "flying saucers." I had been interested in them since junior high school. My late mother would bring home books from the library for us to read and discuss; sort of a mother-son book club. At first, it was comedy books: P. G. Wodehouse, H. Allen Smith, Robert Benchley. Next, it was science fiction books: Isaac Asimov, Ray Bradbury, Robert Heinlein. Then, one day, it was flying saucer books: Major Donald Keyhoe, George Adamski, Frank Scully (whose surname would much later be appropriated for the X-Files). I was hooked!

At that time, WOR Radio in New York broadcast a late-night program hosted by "Long John" Nebel, and it was filled with UFO stories — or, rather, interviews. Nebel (I imagined him sitting there in his long johns) would bring on a disc devotee, allow him to spin his preposterous yarn, then turn loose his panel of skeptics to rip him to shreds. Except, I often came away believing the story, despite the best efforts of actor Khigh Dhiegh — the original Wo Fat in *Hawaii Five-0;* Dr. Walter Martin — the "Bible Answer Man;" and James Randi — the world's most infamous and obnoxious debunker.

I subscribed to *Sky and Telescope* magazine. I joined, and became the president of, the school Astronomy Club, and even gave the planetarium lectures (yes, our school actually had its own planetarium!). I bought a 2.4-inch refracting telescope and searched the heavens from my tiny front lawn. One day, my star-gazing paid off when I spotted a genuine UFO! That experience formed the backbone of my debate with Jesse.

Meanwhile, Jesse had become president of the Chess Club and beaten everyone in the school. Seeking new heights to conquer, he joined the Debate Club. I attended one meeting, but was intimidated by the ravenous future lawyers who feasted on fresh meat like me. I watched one debate and never came back. Jesse, however, stayed and wound up on the interscholastic debate team (he was part carnivore).

Now about our contest. The teacher explained the rules of the debate, and started it rolling: "First up, Mr. Jesse Goodrich." Jesse, all five foot five of him, stood before our class of young overachievers and read from a neatly typed script. "Resolved," he began, "that UFOs are not supportable by science, common sense, or even sanity." I felt his sharp incisors on my jugular vein.

He started out with science. "Where's the evidence — grainy photographs which could be anything, or clear ones which are obvious fakes? How do you explain the impossible aerobatics: G-forces which would kill anyone on board and the unbelievably high speeds? Why hasn't a single reputable scientist come forth to support these wild claims? Because they are just that: scientists, not pseudo-scientists."

Then, with surgical precision, he went to common sense. "So, you would have us believe that an alien race has the courage to embark on interplanetary travel, yet is too shy to say hello when they get here?"

Then, the *coup de grâce*: sanity. "The simple explanation, which is almost always the correct one, is that these saucerian spectators are merely manifesting the latest form of societal psychosis."

I have to admit, he had good arguments. But even more important, he had amazingly affected alliteration. There was a smattering of applause. The teacher just smiled wryly and called my name. "Next up, Mr. Wade Davis."

I stood up, all stocky six feet of me, and unfolded a hand-scrawled five pages of notes, which I had hastily authored that morning while on the 59 trolley car.

"Resolved," I began, "that flying saucers are real and extraterrestrial." I had the class's attention, even if they were looking at me a bit askew.

"If you don't look up," I went on, "chances are you will never see a flying saucer. If you do look up, and happen to see one, your view of the world will be changed forever. For one thing, you'll know how the government constantly lies about the subject.

"I. Looked. Up. And noticed that one of the stars in the constellation of Cygnus the Swan was brighter than it was supposed to be. Way brighter. So, I dragged one of our Adirondack chairs onto the front lawn, sat down in the bitter cold, and continued looking up. In one of my beloved saucer books, I had read that UFOs sometimes parked in front of bright stars, so no one would notice them. No one, it turned out, except a certain saucer enthusiast on his frigid front lawn.

"Nothing happened for about twenty-odd minutes. So, out of desperation, I tried to get into telepathic communication. 'Show yourself!' I commanded. 'Show yourself!' After a while, my intention was rewarded: the bright star started moving verrry slowly from its position, revealing the actual star at its correct brightness. It paused for a second; it accelerated, leaving a bright trail; and then it blinked out.

"It was not swamp gas, as there were no swamps within thirty miles. It was not a weather balloon, as there were no weather stations in suburban Philadelphia. It was not mass hysteria, as there was no mass, just unhysterical me. None of the usual, shop-worn explanations applied — because it was an extraterrestrial vehicle, checking out the Philly suburbs. How did I know? Because, a few days later, at twilight, it returned — this time being chased by a jet from Willow Grove Naval Air Station. I ran into my house to get my 8mm movie camera and returned just in time to film the jet streaking by about sixty feet above my house. When I got the film back from the lab, I looked carefully for any sign of the UFO — but I had just missed filming it, although the jet was clearly visible. Thus, my evidence is one of logic: we don't usually scramble jets to chase gas, balloons, or delusions — or our own aerial vehicles.

"I've seen other unidentified flying objects, but most of them could not be certified as genuinely extraterrestrial. Some of them made crazy turns and were probably real-deal saucers, but I couldn't be certain. Maybe the reason you haven't seen one yourself... is that you don't look up!"

I took my seat. In my opinion, I had topped Jesse, because I was an actual eyewitness. Nevertheless, my speech was received with an awkward silence, punctuated with a few muffled giggles. And when the class voted, I was soundly defeated. In fact, I didn't receive a single vote. I had to accept the bitter truth — that UFOs were imaginary and I should have stuck with P. G. Wodehouse.

II. College

College! All of us had expected Jesse to explode in academia like some scholastic supernova wherever he went. He had numerous scholarship offers, which is not unusual for someone with perfect SATs and a 101% grade point average. Yes, you read it correctly, 101%. As members of an advanced placement class, we all had three points added to our averages, and Jesse — with his 98% — needed only two points to score a perfect 100. But they gave him the gratuitous 1% anyway. Consequently, he had his choice of any college in the world! Harvard lusted after him, as did other Ivy League schools, especially the local University of Pennsylvania. But, for some unfathomable reason, Jesse chose the University of Nevada, Las Vegas!

What?!

Now, don't get me wrong. UNLV is a fine school — blah, blah, disclaimer, disclaimer — but it's no Princeton or Yale. Its motto is *"Omnia Pro Patria* — All for Our Country,"* which offered some sort of clue. Jesse had always been a vocal patriot, who delighted in challenging our fashionable adolescent cynicism. He seemed to believe the official, government line on everything. The fact that UNLV's mascot was a Confederate Rebel somehow did not faze him at all. So, contrary to all rational expectations, Jesse rejected ivy and embraced sagebrush.

As for me, I went to Drexel Institute of Technology and studied Mechanical Engineering so I could design advanced aircraft. I wanted to build one that could exhibit the aeronautical characteristics of the aircraft which (I imagined) I had seen above my childhood home. My bedroom was covered in airplane photographs, which I had requested from Lockheed, Northrop, Bell, and every other company with a decent PR department. I had a model airplane hanging from my chandelier. And I had a TWA sticker on my closet door. These planes were the latest technology — or so I believed at the time.

My college career was unremarkable, so I won't bore you with the details. The only significant event occurred in analog computer lab, when my partner Jack Richter and I inserted a circuit board into the aging machine, and instead of a graph, it produced a plume of black smoke. The school tried to contact the manufacturer for repair, but the company had gone out of business years before. In fact, there were no companies that repaired analog computers. So, Jack and I shared the distinct honor of forcing Drexel into the Digital Age, marked by the purchase of a spanking new IBM 1620. Try as we might, however, no matter what our decks of punch cards contained, there was never any black smoke to reward our efforts.

Even though I had more than enough credits to graduate, I took a digital computing course as an elective, figuring that there might be a future in it, and it just may be helpful in aeronautical design (good guess!).

This was the dawning of the age of computerization, so things were remarkably primitive. The instructor (whose name, ironically, was Decima), would give us a simple problem, which we would flowchart and translate into Fortran II code. Then we would patiently wait our turn at the keypunch machine, and enter the dozen-or-so lines into 80-column cards. Next, we would submit the card deck over the counter to the computer operator, who would add it to his stack of student jobs. The next day, we would pick up our deck along with a printout, on which most of the time, in fuzzy, misregistered capital letters, was the word "ERROR." Alas, this new technology was not going to help me build a spaceship, any more than our burnt-out analog computer would have.

Speaking of spaceships, the 1960s saw the popularization of alien abduction stories. It all started with the infamous Betty and Barney Hill case in 1961, as detailed in their book *The Interrupted Journey*. It then grew into a regular phenomenon reported by an increasing number of so-called "abductees."

The Hills experienced something called Missing Time. Their 178-mile drive should have taken about four hours, but they arrived home seven hours after their departure. Under hypnosis, they discovered that the three missing hours were allegedly spent aboard an alien craft! Other abductees claimed to have had similar experiences.

I paid no attention to these obvious fictions. I may have been a UFO true believer, but I had my limits. And there was no way I would fall for this insanity. Actually, it was comforting to have something to *not* believe in, and it helped my self-image to possess a tiny modicum of skepticism.

III. Young Man in L.A.

I graduated with a Bachelor's degree in Mechanical Engineering and stayed on to obtain a Master's degree to make myself more employable. Then I immediately moved to California, where the aerospace industry was centered. I found an apartment in Hollywood and made new friends — who were nothing at all like the ones I had in Philly.

One new friend told me that, when he was on LSD in Big Sur, he saw a UFO land and three creatures alight from it to collect seawater; he saluted them, and they saluted back! Another friend, stoned on Acapulco Gold, saw a rocket ship passing silently in the sky above a bus stop on Franklin Avenue, leaving a trail of bright green sparks! A third friend, while on magic mushrooms, observed a mailman morph into a praying mantis-shaped alien, who then flew off in his rotating USPS Jeep. I flashed on my high school English class, wondering how my classmates would have greeted these eyewitness reports. Jesse would have won any debate with them without uttering a word.

My California friends' anecdotes were hardly the stuff of scientific rigor, but they were a refreshing change from calculating wing lift coefficients and other mundane engineering endeavors. My employment applications went into a desk drawer. I reasoned (or rationalized) that my aerospace career could be put on hold while I broadened my experience with more subjective realities.

Michael David Wadler

I had always sought to discover an extraterrestrial connection in outer space via astronomy. However, here in L.A., that was no longer an option, as the city's perpetual haze obscured every star in the sky. Sadly, a fleet of giant, mile-long motherships could be hovering directly above us, and we would be none the wiser. So, I parked my outer space interests, substituting an exploration of inner space. After all, it was the Sixties — and, like my new friends, I was young and stupid.

To inaugurate my new avocation, I put on my favorite Rolling Stones album, gobbled down some orange Owsley LSD, and dove headlong into my first round of psychedelic roulette. By the time the album ended, Mick was no longer very lonely 2,000 light years from home — because I was there too, accompanying him on air guitar.

Over the ensuing months, I cycled through every piece of space music at Sam Goody's record store. One day it was David Bowie's "Space Oddity." Another, it was Neil Young's "After the Gold Rush." I even tripped to the Bonzo Dog Band's "I'm the Urban Spaceman." But when I dropped a tab of acid and put on Frank Sinatra's "Fly Me to the Moon," the neighbors complained, so I was forced to finish my trip outdoors.

I proceeded east on Franklin Avenue, pausing at every bus stop to gaze upward — hoping against hope to see a rocket ship leaving a trail of bright green sparks. No such luck. Eventually, this led me to a park in Hollywood called Fern Dell. I followed the long and winding road, which was a much-too-steep nature trail. At one point, an enormous spidery-thing walked past me. I said, "Hello, tarantula," and she replied, "Hello, hippie." Good acid.

It took, I would estimate, about three days to make it to the top of the hill. But it was worth every moment, because there — in all its cinematic glory — stood the Griffith Observatory! It possessed all the unreality of every movie location I had ever visited, so for a while I was James Dean in *Rebel Without a Cause,* trying to talk some sense into Sal Mineo — while *Flesh Gordon* was shooting his sex-ray at Dale Ardor, even though that softcore porn flick wouldn't be produced for another two years.

I followed the crowd and found myself in a familiar place — inside a planetarium! But this wasn't a high-school-sized one, this was city-sized! I leaned back, and gazed at Cygnus the Swan, looking for a star that was brighter than it was supposed to be. They were all the correct magnitude, but they did form an undulating backdrop for the massive Klingon Battle Cruiser (visible only to me) which strafed the audience.

When the presentation ended, I crawled out from under my seat and, per orders, proceeded to the gift shop, where I purchased a star map. You can buy one of these anywhere in Hollywood, but this one was of the sky, not Beverly Hills and environs (in those days, the movie stars were doing so many drugs, they often needed to buy maps to their own homes).

On the way back down the hill to Fern Dell, I remembered that I had arachnophobia and hurried past the tarantula. I hoped she wouldn't notice and be offended — but I swear I heard an ethnic slur hurled in my direction with a heavy insectoid accent. How she knew I was half Jewish is anybody's guess.

My surrealistic existence continued unabated, fueled by various mind-altering compounds. I pretty much forgot my original objectives in coming to L.A. — in fact, I forgot all of my objectives in life. Gone were the aerospace career, ufology fascination — and surfing, which I had not yet gotten around to trying. But I was having more adventures than I ever had and didn't want them to end. As long as my savings account held up, there was no reason to straighten up and get a job.

Then one day, while scarfing down a jar of Nutella, I happened to glance out my window and saw my next-door neighbor Sheila's stereo equipment and TV set being loaded onto a pickup truck — but not by Sheila. I could swear it was being done by another neighbor, a malevolent speed-freak named Gonzo who lived in the Casa Argyle. Later that day, when Sheila knocked on my door to ask if I knew what had happened to her prized electronics, I fingered Gonzo. When His Malevolence heard what I had done, he pounded on my door, claiming he was innocent and threatening to kill me. And I knew he meant it, because he was waving a gun!

I crawled out the bathroom window and hurried down to Hollywood Boulevard, where I lost myself in the crowd. My acid-addled mind could only come up with one plan: you need a disguise! I went into Hollywood Toy looking for something suitable. Rejecting the impulse to buy an alien mask, I bought a fake beard and dark glasses. Then I went a few doors down to The Supply Sergeant to buy fatigues. I spent the next few hours wandering up and down Hollywood Boulevard, a bearded, myopic, faux war vet contemplating his poor life choices.

At about 3:00 AM, I snuck back to my apartment and crawled back through the bathroom window. Without turning on any lights, I grabbed a pillow and blanket, lay down in my closet for a few winks, and fell into a deep, troubled slumber.

I dreamed I saw silver space ships flying in what looked like the yellow haze of the sun. Suddenly, Neil Young's dream was interrupted by the sound of someone crawling through my bathroom window (most likely protected by a silver spoon). I opened my Boy Scout penknife, pointed it at the door, and held my breath. The door opened abruptly — and there stood Sheila! "What's with the beard, Wade?" she inquired. Apparently, the disguise didn't fool her.

"Gonzo's trying to kill me," I whispered. "Don't tell him I'm here!"

"Not to worry, man," she replied. "He's cool. My stuff was ripped off by someone who looks like him. All speed-freaks look pretty much alike: sunken cheeks, twitchy eyes, droopy mustaches. There's one apartment in the Casa that looks like it's being rented by identical, anorexic quintuplets. (That chick could really turn a phrase!) Gonzo got back all my stuff."

"Really?" I cried, overcome with relief. "Then he's not going to murder me?"

"Not over my stuff," she replied reassuringly. "In fact, he feels bad that he scared you and wants to make it up to you."

And he did. As a peace offering, he went to Sam Goody's and stole me the soundtrack album of *2001, a Space Odyssey*. It's always nice to have a backup copy.

My take-away from this incident: drugs are not a reliable way to increase perception, analysis, or judgement. Drugs are fucked-up! So, I did them for only another two years. And had fun times with Sheila, as well as her friends Shauna and Shannon, whom I referred to collectively as the "shtoner shisters." After all, it was the Shixties.

Then one October evening, while alone in the desert, far removed from the city lights, I found myself gazing up at the nighttime sky. It had been a long time since I had indulged in this simple pleasure. Too long. The Milky Way was so brilliant, it kind of scared me! "The stars were never this bright over Philly," I said to myself, noting that this would make a serviceable lyric for a country-western tune.

Other, deeper thoughts, followed. I realized that whatever truth I had been looking for in inner space just wasn't there to be found. And if I didn't get back to my original purpose, I might never do so. Was I that curious kid on his front lawn, or a hopeless druggie? The prospect of a wasted life, after all I had invested in an aerospace career, shocked me into sobriety. I had things to do! And number one on the list, when I got home, was flushing my stash down the toilet. Thank you, Milky, for the intervention, and for showing me the Way! I was still young, but a little less stupid.

IV. Employment

After my extended period of self-indulgence and debauchery, I opened the desk drawer and removed the applications for work at local aerospace companies. I applied to a half dozen and was accepted by all of them (shades of Jesse Goodrich!). I narrowed it down to a toss-up between Lockheed in Burbank and Douglas in Long Beach. I opted for the pleasing irregularity of mountains over the harsh orthogonality of gantry cranes. But mainly, I had heard stories about a special facility at Lockheed known as the Skunk Works, where super-advanced technology was being developed. That's where the U-2 was born (the American spy plane, not the Irish rock group). There were rumors circulating of even more advanced designs with extraordinary capabilities.

It turned out that life at Lockheed was a real trip — a boring one, working on a mundane commercial airliner project. But there were advantages. In those days, aerospace jobs were a license to print money. My expense account was almost as large as my salary, and almost everything I bought was expensed. That helped soften the monotony of being a Junior Engineer I, which was a step above Girl Coder (as they were called during those unenlightened times — no kidding!).

My personal project was designing restroom signage for the L-1011 Tristar. That early wide-body plane was famous for its rattling take-offs and landings, due to the fact that Lockheed used shims instead of precision tooling. Shims are pieces of metal that are wedged into an opening that wouldn't exist if the adjacent parts had been machined correctly. Overall, only 250 L-

1011s were sold, and it was considered an economic failure, badly overshadowed by the tightly-built Boeing 747 series. In fact, after the L-1011 program ended, Lockheed concentrated exclusively on military aircraft.

I asked my boss, Jim Crozier, if I could be reassigned to something more cutting-edge — a plane that didn't rattle like an old-west buckboard, and performed more like a UFO — broadly hinting that the Skunk Works would be a good fit. I pictured myself working alongside such legends as Kelly Johnson and Ben Rich, who were world-class aeronautical visionaries.

Jim just laughed. There was no way I could qualify, he advised, due to my lack of experience. But he let me fill out an application, a thirty-page monster that basically asked me to chronicle, in exhaustive detail, how I had spent every moment of my twenty-eight years on Planet Earth. It was worth a shot. Also, I put in a lot of overtime, even double overtime, in the hope that I would rise to the level of Junior Engineer II, which would be a baby-step closer to my dream job.

The overtime, unfortunately, took its toll on my favorite avocation. I spent less and less time reading about our extraterrestrial visitors, until my obsession started to fade, much like that pseudo-star I had observed above my home all those years ago. In fact, my obsession nearly blinked out. Then, one day, I received a survey from the prestigious American Institute of Aeronautics and Astronautics. It contained one question: "Do UFOs represent a scientifically significant phenomenon?" Maybe there were others out there like me!

I answered "certainly," and was thrilled to learn later that 23% of the responses agreed with mine. That's not all: 30% said "probably" and 27% "possibly." Only 20% had responded "probably not" or "certainly not." I was part of the 80% who took UFOs seriously! My obsession was rekindled!

I figured it was time to meet up with some of these like-minded individuals. But where did they hang out? I did some research and came up with an organization named MUFON — the Mutual UFO Network. It had been around for many years and had a great reputation — as well as a terrible reputation, depending on whom you asked. What attracted me most was the word "mutual." I was majorly in need of a large dose of mutuality.

The first meeting I attended impressed me greatly. Although composed of volunteers, the people were very professional and seemed to care about their mission — which was to investigate UFO sightings, offering an open mind and sympathetic ear. This was in stark contrast to the government-run Project Blue Book, whose obvious purpose was to explain away all valid sightings. MUFON members often referred to Blue Book as "Blah Book."

The meeting was chaired by the chapter president, Dudley Banks, who bore a striking resemblance to the Assistant Dean of Men at Drexel Tech. Consequently, I took an immediate dislike to him. Dudley called on various members to present reports on investigations they had recently conducted.

One member read from a sheaf of forms which he had filled out while meeting with someone who had seen a cylindrical "mothership" in the sky above the Mojave Desert. Apparently, the cylinder had remained perfectly still for about five minutes, and then took off like a bullet. The audience was very receptive, a few members reinforcing the narrative with their own similar experiences.

A second member delivered a short speech on the Billy Maier phenomenon, complete with high-definition photographs of a circular UFO which resembled a wedding cake. Maier was a Swiss farmer who claimed to have met personally with extraterrestrials of the blond, Nordic type. The audience was split down the middle on the veracity of the report. To me, his photos were too "on the nose," although I admit it could have been jealousy over his precise photography, as opposed to my own sloppy videography.

The third member impressed me more than the others: a woman named Tina Ellsworth, who gave a field report augmented by images from a clunky old Kodak Carousel projector. The slides were supposed to document impressions made by a small flying saucer's landing gear, but the three marks could just have easily been indentations from a Weber barbecue grill. The so-called evidence didn't prove a thing, but I didn't care. What I cared about was Tina Ellsworth.

In addition to being beautiful and vivacious, she was obviously very intelligent and mature. But, more than that, there was just something... special about her. My recent experience had been with "shtoners," who were strictly young hippie chicks (not that I had deserved any better). They spoke in nasal, little girl voices, but Tina had a grown woman's mellifluous tones. What a difference!

Watching her, I thought to myself: *I'm done playing around with kids. I want one of those.* However, this particular one appeared to be out of my league. Plus, she seemed awfully chummy with President Banks, and I pegged them as a couple. Consequently, I didn't even bother to speak with her.

MUFON was an important first step back on my path. The second was signing up for a fledgling UFO conference, to be held in Roswell, New Mexico, one of the sacred shrines of ufology. For the uninitiated, this was the location of the first popularized UFO crash in 1947. The city had since done a thriving tourist business. UFO souvenirs were for sale everywhere, giving fresh meaning to the term "space junk."

My trip was like a religious pilgrimage, in which I was surrounded by fellow believers, all looking to confirm their belief in the unbelievable. I wondered how many of them had a master's degree in aeronautical engineering, and how many were just simple-minded rubes fascinated by high strangeness. Mostly the latter, I figured. To blend in, I removed my Drexel class ring, as soon as my trusty Ford Falcon entered the city limits, and I wished that I still had that disguise from my Hollywood Boulevard misadventure.

I checked into the Roswell Inn, mainly because of their clever slogan, "Crash Here." I toured the sights (in the hot, barren desert, where they sold bottles of ice-cold Jupiter Juice). I bought a few self-published pamphlets on fringe sciences, such as electrogravitics and free energy. And I attended a lecture by someone who badly needed a course in public speaking. He was way below the competence level of MUFON. But I did come away having learned about the major division in ufology, which was threatening to become an actual schism: are they ours (built by Earthlings) or theirs (built by, what, Spacelings)? As the speaker clearly stated it: "We, like, don't really, um, know, I mean, like whose they are. So... like..."

I was certain that what I had seen from my front lawn couldn't have been "ours." I wondered if there even was an "ours." If there were, maybe that's what was being engineered at the Skunk Works. My head was spinning with the possibilities.

I did learn something useful: that there was something called a "bulletin board system," or BBS, where users could dial in from their personal computers and post messages on any subject, even UFOs. All I needed was a personal computer and a dial-up modem, whatever that was. I made a mental note to research this arcane technology when I got home.

The time flew by in Roswell. I have to admit that it was an enlightening three days. But when I drove home from that fateful pilgrimage, time did more than fly by: one third of it disappeared! My sixteen-hour road trip took twenty-four hours, and I had no recollection of where those missing eight hours went.

Missing time? Oh, no! I didn't believe in alien abductions! Yet, like Betty and Barney Hill, I had experienced the major symptom of one. My self-imposed limit as a UFO true believer had been breached! Not only that, my sturdy Timex wristwatch had died, and I had a strange lump in my left wrist, which wasn't there before. Was it an implant, or merely a mosquito bite? Only time and Calamine lotion would resolve the mystery.

V. Regression

The lotion reduced the lump, but it still felt like something foreign — need I say alien? — was under my skin. I didn't remember anything about any abduction, and it would be many years before I discovered what had actually happened to me. In the meantime, I remained blissfully ignorant. Nevertheless, my life changed dramatically.

For one thing, I was compelled to sell my Ford Falcon and buy a used Triumph TR3B. I was never a sports-car aficionado, and didn't particularly appreciate British engineering, so this was very strange behavior (or should I say "behaviour?"). I even bought the owner's manual and joined a users' group, which was headquartered halfway around the bloody globe. I named my car Astra, which is Latin for Star. I had never before felt the need to name a car.

For another thing, I became obsessed with studying about esoteric Nazi technology, especially the Vril Society, which claimed to have pioneered anti-gravity propulsion using a device known as *"Die Glocke,"* or The Bell (if they had it, then why didn't Hitler use it in WWII?).

And, for some reason, solar astronomy became a major preoccupation. I bought and read every book under the Sun about the Sun. I became positively obsessed with our bright yellow dwarf. My favorite Beatles song became

Michael David Wadler

Here Comes the Sun, and my favorite Beatle became George (sorry, Ringo).

All of this was very weird, even for me. I began to worry that I was suffering the after-effects of my druggie days. I decided to find a good hypnotist and get to the bottom of the mystery.

By "good hypnotist," I meant one who wouldn't feed me false memories to make a name for himself. To be certain of this, I wanted someone who didn't believe in UFOs. Also, I wanted someone who didn't practice standard hypnosis. The dictionary defines that process as "putting someone to sleep," which is right there in the root of the word (ὑπνος, Greek for "sleep"). I wanted someone who would take me back in time fully awake, and let me speak about what I found, without any sneaky suggestions. I wanted a regressor. Was that even a thing?

There were no listings in the Yellow Pages for regressors, so I scouted around the Therapists section in the hope that something would pop out. Sure enough, there was an eighth-page ad for a Dr. Justin Barbeau, NDNJRT (non-directive, non-judgmental regression therapist). In L.A., anyone can put up a shingle and practice anything. I made an appointment for a consultation.

Barbeau's office was strictly low-rent, situated above a Thai restaurant in a Glendale mini-mall. I found it reassuring that he was so low-profile. His diploma (from the Mesmer Institute of Manitoba) was dated only two years prior, so he was a newbie. In the waiting room, I looked carefully at his magazine selection, which included *Time, Life,* and *Scientific Canadian;* no copy of *UFO Monthly* in sight!

There was a pamphlet describing the basics of NDNJRT. I scanned it eagerly and discovered to my delight that he would simply send me back, and I would report what I found. He would be more of a guide than a commander. So far so good. I figured he was young and hungry — but, then, so was I, as the smells from the restaurant below me caused visions of *pad thai* to dance in my head.

The good doctor greeted me warmly, with just the slightest hint of desperation. We discussed cost and I got directly to the point: "What do you think about UFOs?" His answer totally disarmed me: "I have no idea — but if they're real, are they ours or theirs?" Jackpot!

The supposed consultation turned into an actual session. I sat in a comfortable, second-hand lounge chair (by the looks of it, a Salvation Army rescue), and we began. At last, I would find out what happened to those missing hours!

"What can I do for you?" he asked.

I replied, "Help me find out what happened during my missing time."

"When was this, eh?"

"Last April, the tenth, I believe."

"Let's go there, shall we?"

"How do I do that?" I inquired.

"Close your eyes, and repeat to yourself 'Where's my missing time? Where's my missing time?'"

I did as he asked, and after about fifty repetitions, I was startled to find myself upside-down, gazing at a man in a white smock and a surgical mask, who held me up by my feet and slapped my butt. "It's a boy, Mrs. Davis" he declared. "Nurse, please record the time."

"Holy shit!" I exclaimed, and opened my eyes very wide. "I was looking for nine missing hours, not nine missing months! Is this supposed to happen?"

Barbeau was just as startled. "Heck, no. I've never heard of anyone being regressed to birth." He grabbed a textbook from a shelf and paged through it furiously. "Ah-hah," he finally exclaimed. "By any chance, have you used any psychedelics recently?"

I sheepishly admitted that I had and listed a dozen or more types. He replied that, according to the literature, NDNJRT couldn't produce an accurate result, since my brain was fried like — well, so much *pad thai.* Somehow, he managed to state that fact non-judgmentally (props to the MI of M).

"Can't we try again?" I pleaded. "Please!"

Dr. Barbeau shook his head and said, "Sorry, I can't help you, Mr. Davis. No charge, eh?"

All that I had received for my troubles was the knowledge that I had been born at 2:36 PM, delivered by a short, stocky doctor with a Philadelphia accent. Sadly, I descended down the stairs and drowned my disappointment in *tom kha* soup. This was going to be more difficult than I had imagined. Maybe I should have started with the wrist "implant" — which seemed to wiggle ever so slightly when I added chili to my soup. No mosquito bite had ever acted that way.

VI. Subluxations

It was approaching ten years since my high school graduation, so naturally there was a reunion in the works. I received a sign-up notice from the alumni association. Attached was list of missing graduates, one of which jumped out at me: Jesse Ulysses Goodrich.

Doing my part for my alma mater, I sent him a letter c/o the University of Nevada, Las Vegas. In the letter, I brought him up to date on my successes, totally ignoring the failures (as is common around ten-year reunion time). I asked him what he was doing nowadays, and if there was some way he could make it to the reunion, because I would like to continue our Great Debate, albeit privately (my MUFON files would certainly get the better of him).

Then I went about trying to find a doctor who would remove the lump from my wrist. This was due as much to curiosity, as to eliminating the annoyance when eating spicy food. Plus, it occasionally throbbed. Did this mean that I was actively being monitored? Or (eek!) controlled?!

First, I considered trying the HMO provider under Lockheed's medical plan. But I was concerned they might report my condition to my boss. Jim might have second thoughts about sponsoring an employee for the Skunk Works, if that employee was under alien control.

I briefly tried the Yellow Pages phone directory, but there were so many listings, I couldn't make up my mind. Then I consulted *The Recycler.* Ah-hah! There was an ad for a chiropractor in the MacArthur Park area who proudly proclaimed that he provided X-ray services. I called and made an appointment.

Dr. Clarence Heller's waiting room was like a library of ancient chiropractic literature. By ancient, I mean dating back to chiropractic's founder, D. D. Palmer, who believed that misalignments (aka "subluxations") of the vertebrae could cause almost every disease known to man. Heller proudly displayed pamphlets which touted cures for everything from asthma to irritable bowel syndrome. It seemed odd that someone so steeped in retro treatments would have an X-ray machine, but that was only one of his paradoxes.

Clarence (he insisted that I address him by his first name) greeted me with a crushing handshake, one that I would have expected from someone half his age (which would have been twice mine). "What seems to be the problem, young man?" he inquired.

"I came here to find out what's wrong with my left wrist," I replied. "But now I also need an adjustment for a pulverized right hand."

To his credit, he laughed heartily. "Not bad for an old coot like me, huh? Diet, exercise, and total abstention from worldly vices."

"I love worldly vices," I replied. "They're my favorite kind."

This time there was no laugh, just a wrinkly scowl. Apparently, I had struck one of the coot's nerves. Perhaps he needed an adjustment.

"Let's have a look at that wrist," he offered abruptly. Then he pressed, prodded, and palpated the spot, while I hoped that somewhere an alien wearing headphones was recoiling painfully from loud static. *Serves the little green bastard right,* I thought to myself.

"There's something in there," Clarence advised. "How did this happen?"

"It just appeared there last April. While I was driving in the desert. Calamine lotion brought the swelling down."

He looked at me askance. "Spontaneously, huh?"

"One day it wasn't there, and the next day it was."

"Hmm. Let's pop it in the fryer, and see what we can see." He directed me towards his vintage X-ray machine, which could have once belonged to Marie Curie.

"This is the fryer?" I asked fearfully.

"I'd never use it on myself," he volunteered. "But patients seem to trust it."

I realized why Clarence advertised in *The Recycler.*

He donned a full-length lead apron, which must have weighed a few hundred pounds, and fried up an order of radiocarpal joint.

"It's blurry," he advised. "Like it was moving around. Hmm…"

"Any idea what it is?" I asked. "Some sort of uncharted subluxation?"

"If I were to speculate… Let's just say it's an unknown object of unknown origin and leave it at that."

"Have you ever seen anything like this before?"

"There is nothing like this. That will be seventy-five dollars for the X-rays. Cash. Thanks for coming in." Then he ushered me out, quickly and unceremoniously.

This exchange left me with the distinct impression that he knew exactly what it was and where it came from — and wanted nothing to do with it. Maybe I should take the hint. I left with misgivings, a quivering right hand, and latent radiation burns.

Oh, and my letter to Jesse bounced. A week later, it appeared in my mailbox with a smeared rubber stamp proclaiming: "Unknown Recipient." How could someone as impressive as Jesse be unknown anywhere?

VII. Tina

My phone rang, and a pleasant female voice greeted me. "Wade?"

"Yes, Wade Davis speaking."

"This is Tina."

"Tina?"

"Tina Ellsworth, from MUFON? I gave the presentation at our last meeting."

Wow, that Tina!

"Yeah... oh... sure, I re-remember you," I stammered, with mock casualness.

"As you know, I'm a field investigator. I need a partner for my next project. Dudley suggested that you might be ideal, since you're an engineer."

I didn't want to sound too eager, but out came the words, "I'm your guy!" This was followed instantaneously by a monstrous cringe, accompanied by immense gratitude that picture-phones hadn't yet been invented.

"Great! This is a special one — a low-flying saucer in the Antelope Valley. And the witness has a photo."

Some engineer I was! If the saucer were a passenger transport, I could certainly provide some expertise on its restroom signage. But Tina had no need to know this embarrassing truth. My profession impressed her, and that was enough. Besides, as I understood it, a MUFON investigation was mostly filling out forms.

While awaiting the field trip with nervous anticipation, I figured I'd take another pass at non-hypnotic regression. Since one of my new fascinations was the Vril Society and its allegedly anti-gravitic Bell, or *Glocke*, I arbitrarily decided to find a German therapist. Ideally, the office would be above a *Hofbräu*, so I could drown my likely disappointment in something stronger than soup. Instead, I skipped the first step, and went directly to the Roaring Lion Tavern, to drink good German beer and meditate on my situation. Serving wenches are, as a rule, non-directive and non-judgmental, with the additional advantage of being non-Canadians.

Halfway through my half-liter of *Spaten Optimator*, I started thinking about my drive home from Roswell, New Mexico. Interstate 40 had stretched before me like an endless ribbon of newly poured concrete. On that late April evening, there was hardly any other traffic, and the road seemed to have a hypnotic effect on me (hypnotic!?). I pulled off the highway, followed the signs to a small town, and found myself at a dive bar named the G-Spot (I discovered with disappointment that the "G" stood for "German").

I dimly recalled ordering a bratwurst sandwich and asking for directions to the men's room, which turned out to be outdoors and occupied. So, while I waited, I strolled along... what was it...? A gravel path... and then... nothing. Blackness. A memory hole! Did I ever get to eat that brat?

At the Roaring Lion, finishing up my *Optimator* did nothing to further my recall, and a second one would probably have turned my drive home into a certain DUI. But I was finally making progress on recovering the missing hours. They were located somewhere in or above Flagstaff, Arizona! I tipped Wench Willamina too well (while thinking to myself that she was no Tina), flopped into my TR3B, and managed to navigate Astra home unscathed.

On the day of the Antelope Valley excursion, I drove to Tina's apartment in Studio City and found a parking space a mere two blocks away. I rang her *Glocke*. She opened the door and smiled at me — and for a moment, she was the most beautiful woman in this — or any other — world!

"Hi, Wade. Give me a moment." She went into her bedroom and returned with a sweatshirt flung casually over a shoulder. "It can get pretty chilly in the desert." My body temperature, however, was exceeding that of Death Valley in August.

Even if my overheated physique was not as impressive as it could have been (years of the munchies having taken their toll), I was certain my TR3B would impress her. Sure enough, she commented on it as soon as she saw it. "Wow, I didn't have you pegged as the sporty type!" It was a pretty left-handed compliment, kind of like reminding me I was a dork, but I accepted it with grace and gratitude.

On the way to the interview, we shared our personal UFO experiences. Tina revealed that she and her brother Merrill had seen strange lights in the sky, doing bizarre maneuvers. She had looked up! That had led her to a lifelong fascination with the subject. Merrill, on the other hand, was a die-hard skeptic. "I'll believe in aliens when I meet one, and not a moment before." He had invalidated the evidence right before his eyes. Looking up was not enough for him; like many others, he also needed permission from society at large to believe in anything.

I told her of my UFO history, recounting an edited version of my debate with Jesse that didn't make me look like a complete loser. She seemed genuinely entranced by my narrative, especially about how close the UFO was over my house.

"Wow. Could you see the craft clearly?"

"Not so much," I confessed. "It was more of a round, fuzzy, bright light."

She paused a moment, deep in thought, and then replied, "I think, more than anything, I'd love to see one close up. I mean, really close-up! It's my fondest wish."

"Not too close," I ventured. "There's no telling what the occupants would want with you." That was as near as I dared to go about my possible abduction.

"Where's your sense of adventure, Wade? I'd want to actually touch it!"

It was intoxicating to discuss my experiences with a woman who was at least my intellectual equal. However, our respective subtexts differed markedly: she was sharing information with a coworker, while I was fantasizing that this was our first date — which would end at her place for some liquid refreshment and her possibly touching it. After all, engineer or not, I was still a man.

The interview with the witness went really well. Tina and the old lady, one Molly Andrews, hit it off like old friends. I mostly took notes, filled out forms, and smiled a lot — maybe too much. The photographic evidence turned out to be a Polaroid snapshot of something vaguely circular, but Molly's description of the event (lots of right-angle turns!) was riveting. This may have been because Molly was an English teacher at Palmdale High, and therefore could speak the language fairly competently. She was delighted to find out that Tina taught math at an L.A. inner-city school (oh, if I haven't mentioned this fact up until now, there's a good reason: I didn't know about this up until now! Honestly, I can be such a dork!).

Anyway, Molly simply adored Palmdale High, and Tina hated everything about the L.A. Unified School District. By the end of the interview, Molly had convinced Tina to consider relocating to Palmdale. This was not how I imagined our "first date" would have gone.

On the way back, I did my not-so-subtle best to dissuade her from moving to the Antelope Valley. "It's a hot, insect-and-snake-infested hellhole," I mentioned matter-of-factly. "You'll be ninety minutes away from any culture. And the planes coming in and out of Edwards Air Force Base will keep you awake all night." She didn't argue with me, but I could see I was losing yet another debate.

As night fell, the desert temperature dropped suddenly, which was no match for my TR3B's skimpy heater. Tina squeezed into her sweatshirt, and I was stunned to see the letters "UNLV" (Jesse's *alma mater*), and the motto *"Omnia Pro Patria."* I scored a point with her when I provided the English translation. I'm sure Dudley Banks wasn't half the Latin scholar I was!

I refocused and told her all about Jesse and how he had mysteriously disappeared. It turned out that Tina had a college chum named Elsa Zabotny, the class valedictorian, who had also vanished after graduation. "Maybe they ran off together," I suggested, half kidding. Tina replied, "Elsa wouldn't have run off with a *man*." Another perfectly good theory bites the dust!

Then I had a brilliant idea. "Do you still have your college yearbook?"

"Yes, why?"

"I need to do some research on the University of Nevada, Las Vegas."

She agreed to bring her yearbook to the next month's MUFON meeting. I secretly looked forward to that as our second date.

VIII. Reunions

In the meantime, I flew to my reunion back east on a Boeing 747, which didn't rattle. But the restroom signage, in my professional opinion, was sub-par.

As I mentioned at the start of this reminiscence, Jesse didn't show up. I told the others about my abortive attempt to reach out to him, and we tried to top one another with absurd theories of *God*rich's whereabouts (my Donald Duck theory was underappreciated). I also trumpeted my dubious personal achievements, ignoring anything controversial, especially my MUFON adventures. I was hoping to shed my reputation as the credibility-challenged weirdo who imagined he had seen UFOs. Thankfully, no one brought it up. They were too busy bragging about their burgeoning legal or medical practices (I resisted the urge to ask the latter if they could give me a deal on alien implant removal).

Someone had heard from someone else who heard it on the grapevine that Jesse had majored in astrophysics, with a minor in linguistics. That would be pure Jesse — the overachievers' overachiever! But since no one else in our class had gone to UNLV, there was no further information about him. Nevertheless, even though he was absent, his presence was still strong — so much so that, as usual, Jesse Ulysses Goodrich dominated the event.

On my return, I counted the days until the next MUFON meeting, when I would see Tina and her yearbook, but mostly Tina. She had edged out my older obsession. Meanwhile, I used the time productively to proceed with my BBS plans.

There were many personal computers to choose from, the most prominent of which were the Radio Shack TRS-80, the Apple-1, and the IBM PC. I had heard the TRS-80 referred to as the "TRASH-80" by those in the know. And the Apple machine seemed more like a toy than a professional product. Consequently, I opted for good old IBM. I figured that, like most of corporate America and Drexel Tech, you can't go wrong with IBM. And the PC came with twin floppy disk drives!

Next, I needed a modem, which was the device used to modulate and demodulate the communication signal between the digital computer and the analog telephone lines, hence its name. I learned that the Bell 103 boasted full-duplex transmission and frequency-shift keying. That was good enough for me — since I had no idea what either of those terms meant. Besides, it had a speed of 300 bits per second, which seemed like way more than enough of them.

I spent many frustrating hours hooking things up, with half-a-dozen calls to customer support, but I finally had my rig working. The first time I connected to a BBS, I felt like Alexander Graham Bell must have when placing that first call to his assistant, Thomas A. Watson (no relation to IBM's legendary chief executive, Thomas J. Watson). I logged onto the fledgling bulletin board and was rewarded with a list of topics, slowly displaying one letter at a time. One of them was "Flying Saucers"! I entered the proper combination of keystrokes and *voila!* I was able to read mostly incoherent messages from enthusiastic, but barely literate, fellow zealots. But it was a start!

The long-awaited MUFON meeting finally arrived, and I was very happy to see Tina again. I had arrived early, reserving a seat next to me so she wouldn't have to sit next to Dreadful Dudley. My clever strategy paid off!

Tina handed me a copy of her yearbook, *The Rebel.* I thanked her much too effusively and found myself less captivated by that slim volume than by her fragrance, which I found intoxicating. It was probably only Prell shampoo, but to me, it was ambrosia.

While the chairman babbled on about reported UFO sightings, I thumbed through the yearbook. There was no trace of Jesse in the chess or debate club photos, but that may have been because he had already graduated. Then something strange caught my eye: in the group photo of the Air Force ROTC, there was someone with Jughead-like ears. AFROTC?! Jesse in the military? *Wait till I tell my classmates,* I thought to myself. *I've experienced a genuine, second-hand Jesse sighting!* This was even rarer than a saucer sighting. Maybe it deserved its own BBS mailbox (or whatever the hell they called it).

When the meeting (aka our second date) ended, I asked Tina for a third one. But I artfully disguised it as a field trip to UNLV, to follow up on my Jesse research. "You can also try to track down your friend Elsa Zabowski," I added. She smiled that million-megawatt smile, and replied, "Zabotny."

"I'll take that as a 'yes,'" I said. And from that point on, whenever I needed to say "yes" to Tina, instead I would say "Zabotny." A private language is part of any real relationship, which is what I hoped this would turn out to be.

IX. Wandering in the Desert

We arrived at UNLV during finals week. As I drove around campus, Tina played tour guide, pointing out places that had a special meaning to her. Her excitement would have excited me, had I not already been maxed out excitement-wise. "First stop, the library," she said. I obeyed willingly.

All of the little study booths (or "carrels," as they are called in the library trade) were occupied with preoccupied students, conspicuously overstressed by exams and self-medication (I thanked my lucky stars that I was no longer a slave in academia). We set up shop at a small table.

Tina brought us a stack of old yearbooks, and we began our Goodrich research, not quite knowing what we were looking for. If Jesse Goodrich had graduated in 1976, then his picture and bio should have been under the G's. But the '76 *Rebel* had no record of him. Was it possible that he graduated a year earlier or later? The '75 and '77 books also came up empty.

While we pondered the discrepancy, Tina noticed something strange in the '76 book: The G's went directly from "GL" to "GR." Where were all the "GOs"? Every graduating class has a few Goodmans, Goldbergs, and an occasional Gorecki.

Tina's eyes widened. "Wade, look!"

She pointed to two adjacent pages, numbered 83 and 86. Pages 84, and its obverse 85, were missing! On further inspection, we discovered that the page with the Air Force ROTC photo was also gone. Someone had redacted Jesse!

"Next stop, AFROTC office," I announced, forcefully, hoping she didn't have a thing about bossy men. We wended our way cautiously through the carrels, lest we wake the dozers, or shake up the non-dozers.

The AFROTC officer-in-charge claimed to have no record of any Jesse Goodrich in its ranks. Nor any Elsa Zabotny. Could that have been a Jesse look-alike in Tina's yearbook? His ears indicated otherwise.

"Let's try the Alumni Office," Tina suggested.

The clerk at the Alumni Office flatly refused to provide any corroboration for Goodrich's existence, let alone his matriculation at UNLV. "That's personal and privileged info," she stated officiously. "And private."

"Perfect," I said. "An alliteration trifecta." Jesse would have been impressed.

Undaunted, Tina decided to play her trump card — Dr. Palchek, her favorite physics teacher. Every campus has an especially fun-loving professor, one who's constantly in demand as a chaperone or drinking buddy; it's part of the academic stock company. Daniel Palchek, PhD, was UNLV's version. Tina had chuckled her way to an A grade, while actually comprehending the ordinarily dull, dense subject. "If anyone can tell us about a missing astrophysics major, it's Dr. Dan."

We hurried over to the Physics Building and up to Palchek's office on the third floor. A sign on the door proclaimed: "Danger, 1,000,000 ohms resistance." I pretended to be careful not to touch the doorknob, which earned me a tiny Tina smile. Fearlessly, she tried the knob and found it locked.

"I know where he must be," she said. "Follow me."

To the ends of the Earth, I thought to myself. *And beyond.*

We sprinted to an off-campus commercial mini-mall. At Drexel, we had a favorite watering hole named The Green Trees Tavern, which was lax about enforcing age requirements. The UNLV equivalent was named The Thirsty Cactus. We made it past the security guy who was checking fake IDs and proceeded to a private dining room.

And there sat Professor Daniel Patrick Palchek, PhD, behind a wall of empty beer mugs, holding forth on the subject of torsion fields to a pair of inebriated student admirers. He noticed Tina immediately.

"Ah, Ms. Ellsworth!" he exclaimed. "Delighted to see you again."

"Likewise, Dr. Dan!" she responded.

He looked at me quizzically. "I don't recognize you, young man. Were you in one of my classes?"

"No," I replied. I'm not a UNLV grad. I went to Drexel Institute of Technology."

"Never heard of it!" he retorted. "Is it accredited?"

Tina chuckled at his witticism, and I got tongue-tied trying to formulate a snappy comeback.

Palchek just smiled. "Join the celebration!"

"Thanks, we'd love to," said Tina. We sat.

"These disreputable gentlemen are two of my favorite brown-nosers, Mark Zaccard and Mark Marinowitz."

"Nice to meet you," she replied. "This is my colleague, Wade Davis."

Colleague?! Not even friend? That stung, but I tried not to show it.

"What are you celebrating, Professor?" I inquired.

"My final Final, Dave," he replied. Before I could correct my name, he hurtled on. "I'm retiring. Finally."

"Oh, no!" Tina protested.

One of the Marks attempted to say something clever, but after way too many beers, all that emerged was, "Our lawsh is gain's... whatever..." The other Mark nodded in sage agreement.

"What are you planning to do with yourself?" Tina inquired.

"Write that goddamned book, the one I've been threatening to write most of my so-called career."

A waitress appeared, and I turned my attention to the menu. The Thirsty Cactus Special was bratwurst (was the Universe trying to tell me something?). I ordered one with a dark German beer. The wurst that can happen, I punned to myself, would be indigestion and flatulence. The best would be a resumption of recalling the remainder of my personal *Interrupted Journey*. "And another round for everyone!" I added.

"None for ush," said one of the Marks. "We got amother 'xam in (hic) tem minutes."

Palchek continued his lecture. "Like I was saying, all physics taught in schools today is either that brain-dead Newtonian pablum, or that improbable quantum horseshit. The real breakthroughs will occur from rotational physics. Spinning objects do not strictly obey either Newtonian or quantum laws. But where are the research dollars to experiment with torsion fields?"

Where, indeed! My guess was funding the Skunk Works.

"I'll tell you where," the prof answered himself. "Hidden in a black budget, that's where!" Great minds.

He went on to discuss basic Vril technology, and its offshoot, the Thomas Townsend Brown effect. "Get an object spinning fast enough, with a positive plate on top and negative plate on the bottom..." (He demonstrated the principle with a convenient pair of dirty dishes.) "And *voila!* The container acts like a giant condenser, with a mass reduction of about ninety percent — and it levitates! (He tossed the dishes into the air, but they stubbornly refused to remain there.) His facts were reminiscent of the electrogravitics pamphlet I had purchased at Roswell.

Our drinks arrived, refueling the irascible academic. The Marks Brothers took the opportunity to make a graceless exit, attempting to hold the door open for each other, until they simultaneously stepped through the door and collided. "The bombed leading the bombed," observed the good professor. This left Palchek, Tina, me, and the bratwurst, all alone.

"My book is entitled *Forbidden Physics*," Dr. Dan volunteered. "It deals with rotational field effects, as you might have guessed by now. But it also covers the best-kept secret in our science — zero-point energy, also known as free energy."

I nearly choked on my brat.

"People have allegedly died trying to reveal that secret," he declared. "That's supposed to scare away scientists like me. Hah! I figure, fuck it, free energy is too important to keep from the public any longer, when pensioners can't pay their fuel bills. Once people realize that energy can be cheaply extracted from space-time itself, it would mean the end of fossil fuel companies and those goddamn energy monopolies..."

I almost missed that last thing he said, as I had slipped into a reverie of sorts, hearing disembodied voices in my head. They were overlapping, as if a quartet of beings in a UFO were gossiping telepathically about something called...

"Solar Guardian!" I shouted, startling all three of us.

Dr. Dan stopped abruptly and stared at me funny. "What did you say, Dave?"

"I think it was 'Solar Guardian,' sir," I said.

"What do you mean by Solar Guardian?"

"More than you can imagine!" I bluffed. Whatever it meant, it would certainly explain my preternatural obsession with the Sun. I clumsily changed the subject.

"But first, we have a question for you."

There was silence in the room, which seemed to last about half an hour. *We've come this far*, I thought; *it's now or never.*

"We'd like to find out about an alumnus named Jesse Ulysses Goodrich. He seems to have been erased from all school records."

"Ah, yes, one of my Star Pupils."

"You remember him?" I inquired excitedly.

"Who can forget anyone from Operation Star Pupil?"

"Operation...?"

"If you know about Solar Guardian, then you must know about the program to recruit its operatives."

One more lie wouldn't hurt. "Sure!" I continued, guessing wildly. "They recruit them... When they graduate high school. And tell them which college to attend."

Palchek added, "And after graduation, they're sent over to Papoose Lake for advanced training... Oopsie! I think I may have spoken too freely... Forget what I said."

"Totally forgotten, Professor," I reassured him. "By the way, would you have any idea of how I might contact Goodrich? The alumni office wasn't helpful."

"Not a clue," replied the professor. "If you do get in touch, tell that tiresome genius I said hello."

It was time to go. "Thank you so much for your time, Professor. I look forward to reading your book on free energy — if my meager Drexel education is sufficient to comprehend it."

We took our leave, side-stepping broken crockery, as Palchek chugged his sixth beer and ordered a seventh and eighth.

Walking back to my TR3B, Tina complimented me. "Dave, that was absolutely amazing," she said. "Solar Guardian? Where did that come from?"

"I'm not certain," I lied. "Now all we have to do now is figure out what the hell I was talking about. And it's Wade," I added, "not Dave. Wade Davis, your *colleague.*"

Tina looked at me reproachfully. "Honestly, one would think that a man with your sense of humor would be able to take a little teasing!"

I blushed with embarrassment. But at least I knew that she knew who I was. And that she appreciated my strange sense of humor. And enjoyed teasing.

The drive back to L.A. was filled with polite conversation about unimportant matters. But on her way out of my car, she dropped this little bomb. "I've decided to move to the Antelope Valley school district as soon as possible. L.A. Unified sucks way too mightily."

"Will you still be coming to our MUFON meetings?"

"I guess not. The commute would be a killer."

I was crushed, figuring that my conversation with Dr. Dan would have impressed her enough to take our relationship to the next level — i.e., an actual relationship. But it may have scared her away permanently. Another failure — one that truly mattered to me!

Tina must have sensed my disappointment and tried to soften the blow. "I must admit, I'll miss you and our fun excursions. Goodbye, Wade."

"Good night, Thelma," I replied.

She laughed and kissed me tenderly on the cheek. I had bunted and was thrown out at first base. Sigh!

A few days after I returned home, I was shocked to find a letter from Jesse in my mailbox. The envelope was postmarked Parumph, Nevada:

Dear Wade,
I'm sorry I was unable to reply to your letter prior to our ten-year reunion.

Somehow, even though the letter had bounced, he knew its contents!

During that weekend, I was away on special assignment.

As a top-secret operative? Did it have something to do with a new spy plane, I theorized, *something more advanced than the U-2? Perhaps our class's wild speculations were not that far off after all.*

I very much appreciate your interest in my whereabouts. I know you mean well, but I need to tell you that what you're doing is dangerous. Please stop. I can't say any more.

I felt a shiver run up my spine and branch out everywhere there wasn't a subluxation. *I was doing something dangerous? I had never courted danger, being more the studious, and less the heroic, type.* He concluded the letter with:

Who knows? Maybe I'll see you at our fifteen-year reunion.

Sincerely,
Jesse

P.S. There's no need for Great Debate II. You were right after all.

Anyone else reading this letter would have no idea what he was referring to, but I certainly did. Jesse was now a believer in UFOs! Of course! Putting together his cryptic message with Dr. Palchek's inebriated admissions, a picture was beginning to emerge, a very unsettling one.

I signed onto the BBS and created a new topic named "Solar Guardian." As I was composing my message, asking if anyone knew what it meant, the System Administrator changed the topic name to "Terms-of-Use Violation." Totally freaked out, I signed off immediately, unplugged my IBM PC, and dove under my quilt.

For a while, I considered moving back to Philly and my old room, with its comforting non-secret airplane photos. Then I realized that the past few months had been only a bad dream, and what I needed to do was wake up. I stayed up all night trying to wake up and failed miserably at that, too. What to fail at next?

X. Severance

Failing at my job seemed to be the logical next step, and I was right. Jim Crozier called me into his office, with a sour look on his face.

"Wade, I'm afraid I have bad news for you. Your application to the Skunk Works has been rejected, with prejudice."

"With prejudice?" I replied.

"That means…"

"I know what it means," I responded. "Don't bother to reapply."

"It seems that your extracurricular activities are not compatible with working at the SW."

I didn't bother to ask what he meant by "extracurricular."

"What's more," he continued, "I have to ask you to curtail those activities, even while you're working here."

"I have to ask you"? Apparently, he was following a directive from higher up.

"Sure, Jim. I can do that."

He seemed greatly relieved. "Good. I appreciate the work you're doing here and would hate to see it jeopardized."

As nicely as he worded it, I recognized the threat. In my mind, I was already drafting the letter to Dudley Banks, explaining my withdrawal from MUFON. Without Tina, it was no great sacrifice. And I could probably find another BBS — a more private one, with real answers.

And I did. BBSes were popping up all over the place, and I discovered what seemed to be an ideal one: the "No-BS BBS." I joined under an alias ("Dave Colleague"), and posted a topic named "Operation Star Pupil." Then I waited patiently for a nibble on my bait.

Weeks crawled by, and no one responded. At least I wasn't "TOSed" (terminated for a Terms of Service violation). I opened a new thread, "Free Energy" — and man, did that board light up! The only problem was that the posts were mainly rants against Big Power, as well as various related conspiracy theories. Sure, the Rockefellers and Rothschilds were pure Evil, but I was seeking actual data, not fanciful opinions. Apparently, none of my fellow board buddies had been out drinking with Dan Palchek.

Enough of this indirect nonsense, I decided. Caution be damned! And I opened a thread named "Solar Guardian." The following morning, there was a response, from someone named Deep Space: "Do you mean the Secret Space Program?"

The what?! Like everyone else, I had believed that NASA had run our one-and-only space program. There was another, secret one? Is that what this was about? "Sure, the SSP," I lied. "What more can you tell me?"

What he (or she) relayed to me next was so mind-numbing, that all I could do was stare at my screen, trying to absorb what it contained. Here is Deep Space's post, verbatim:

> Solar Guardian is part of a secret space program, staffed by non-terrestrial officers of the U.S. Air Force. It is responsible for monitoring all incoming and outgoing extraterrestrial traffic and defending our solar system. It uses advanced aircraft powered by free energy and propelled by electrogravitics. Presently, it is composed of a few ships, but will eventually have dozens of carriers, fighters, triangular shuttles, and other vessels.

My fascination with all things concerning our sun had come about as a result of my misunderstanding the term "Solar Guardian," which I had heard during my lost-time incident. "Solar" referred to the Solar System!

I printed out a hard copy of the post on my brand spanking new dot-matrix printer, just before the No-BS BBS went down for "unscheduled maintenance." Not surprisingly, it didn't come back up all weekend (uh-oh!).

Monday at work, my mind was somewhere else, and I didn't notice the security officer sitting at my desk until I almost sat on him. He was busy boxing up my personal belongings.

"Mr. Crozier needs to see you," he informed me, sullenly.

Jim smiled a frozen smile, trying to put a happy face on his obviously difficult task. "We really appreciate what you've contributed here," he said. "But it's time that you moved on." He handed me my termination papers, and I was mildly amused to see that the pink slip was actually pink. "Good luck, Wade!"

The security guy escorted me to my car. When he saw what it was, he laughed. "A TR3B? A bit on the nose, isn't it?" I had no idea what he was talking about. Was he a British sports car enthusiast? Was "on the nose" a British automotive-ism expressing disapproval?

"Huh?"

"Everyone knows that TR-3B is the designation of a plane we don't officially make here, and never even heard of," he recited flatly, without a hint of irony.

This was no coincidence. Rather, it was further evidence of what had been buried deep in my subconscious during my disturbing Flagstaff episode.

That evening, while at home, nursing a bottle of Jose Cuervo and pondering my future, I received a call from Tina, who was devastated and in tears. When I was able to calm her down, she gave me the horrible news: "Dr. Palchek has died in a lab accident. Wade, I don't know what to think!"

I did. And it took a lot more tequila to deaden that dark thought.

XI. Men in Sky Blue

Traditionally, UFO witnesses and whistle-blowers are harassed by Men in Black; but I was visited at home by Men in Sky Blue, specifically shade 1620, which is what Air Force officers wear. True to type, both MISBs wore reflective sunglasses, like heavies from a low-budget crime movie. My amusement was short-lived, however, when they began their interrogation.

They wore no nametags and didn't bother to introduce themselves, so I'll refer to them as Officer One (who was a first lieutenant), and Officer Two (who was a second lieutenant). Actually, I had imbibed so much Cuervo, I should have named them *Oficial Uno y Oficial Dos*.

I have tried to leaven this account with humor, but honestly, the encounter shook me to my core. I made a few feeble attempts at joking, but these guys wore side-arms. I never knew that Air Force officers needed to be strapped to interview a harmless civilian. My guess was that it wasn't for protection, it was strictly for intimidation. And it worked.

Officer Two began. "The subject is Operation Star Pupil. What is it you think you know about it? And who have you told?"

"I know nothing about anything called 'Star Pupil,'" I lied. "And while we're at it," I added with uncharacteristic bravado (courtesy of Señor Cuervo), "I know nothing about any Secret Space Program or the Solar Guardian Space Fleet. And it's 'whom have you told,' not 'who have you told.' Thanks for dropping by, flyboys."

If you've never been pistol-whipped, you have no idea how excruciating it can be. In damp weather, my face still hurts.

Officer Two said something he thought was really clever. "Listen, asshole, don't get cute with us." The B-movie dialog matched his methods, as well as his shades.

Officer One, however, was the real thing. He removed his sunglasses, and his eyes narrowed as they focused on me. Very deliberately, he stated: "Sir, please don't trifle with us. We mean business. Unlike your friend Gonzo, from the Casa Argyle." He let that sink in.

I felt a cold shiver from my big toe to the top of my head. He had done his homework and knew all about my sordid psychedelic past. I could see why he was Officer One.

"My partner here doesn't have my patience. But I assure you, we both take our jobs very seriously."

So, in no uncertain terms, it was bad cop, worse cop.

"Make no mistake about it, you are in big trouble. At this moment, we have someone auditing your Lockheed expense account. What do you imagine he will find?"

Hitting me in the face with a government firearm was bad enough, but this went too far. The despotic duo stood and walked toward the door.

"And stay off them bulletin boards!" said Officer Two, while Officer One guaranteed the order by smashing the monitor of my overpriced IBM Model 5150. Through my tears, I watched them drive off in their nondescript motor pool Chevrolet.

I spent the rest of the day alternating between trying to get sober and downing more alcohol. How to deal with my predicament? I came up with a dozen brilliant ideas and rejected all of them as being hopelessly idiotic. Move to Iceland? Have plastic surgery? Boil myself in prune oil? The only idea that made any sense was to write Jesse for advice. After all, he was up to his oversized ears in this matter. So, once again, I sent a letter to him care of UNLV, which had previously claimed not to know him. Maybe it would work again.

The next day, I drove up to Griffith Observatory and looked out at the smoggy city hidden somewhere beneath me. I repeated this ritual day after day, waiting for some glimmer of inspiration. But none arrived. I was truly the fool on the hill.

Finally, I received a reply from Jesse. It consisted of a string of three numbers: one positive, one negative, and one with lots of colons. And there was a two-word Latin admonition: *"Non sectatores!"* followed by a cryptic order: "Then look up!" I passed out in an alcoholic stupor before I could decode the message.

XII. Deus Beatus Ex Machina

In the morning, even with a well-earned hangover, my astronomy training kicked in, and I decoded the three numbers as latitude, longitude, and GMT (Greenwich Mean Time). The Lat-Long described a location about thirty minutes away — a clearing in the San Gabriel Mountains. Then my high school Latin kicked in, and I realized that *non sectatores* meant "no followers." My paranoia doubled.

I left early, to allow for any evasive actions necessary to lose anyone following me. Up a dead-end street. Around the block seven times. Parked by a freeway entrance for twenty minutes. Every time I spotted a car that could have come from a government motor pool, I made a U-turn. No one could have followed me, no matter their espionage expertise!

In spite of the hour that I had spent playing super-criminal, I arrived at the designated location with time to spare. This allowed me to be alone with my thoughts — which was the last place I wanted to be. All I could think about were my too-numerous mistakes and failures, as I surveyed the ruin of my life. I had never felt so lost, alone, and frightened.

When 8:00 PM PST (3:00 AM GMT) rolled around, I looked up. But all I saw were the usual stars at their usual magnitudes. Was this just my latest blunder? I panicked and — as painful as it is to admit — I gave up. And began to be engulfed by a virtual tsunami of self-pity. Why was the Universe (or some sadistic deity) doing this to me?

After what seemed like an eternity, I felt a faint vibration. And, oh so gradually, a dark shape above me began eclipsing a large number of stars. The shape became a triangle! And I was rewarded with the sight of a gigantic black triangular craft hovering silently above me, surrounded by a corona of silvery-blue light. Gracefully and nearly silently, it settled onto the ground.

My heart was beating so fast, I could have been with a trio of Tinas. The hatch opened and — to my utter amazement — an Earthling emerged, his arm around the shoulder of a mid-sized grey alien (who had the physique and pallor of a denizen of Casa Argyle, without the droopy mustache). With a mischievous grin, the Earthling greeted me warmly, "Hi, Fat-Ass!"

After the shock wore off, I responded in kind. "Hey, Jughead. Who's your little friend?" I couldn't help but notice that he bore a striking resemblance to the mask I had rejected at Hollywood Toy.

"He's my cousin," Jesse replied, "a very distant one. Sixty-eight light years removed."

His cousin saluted me smartly, and I awkwardly returned the gesture.

"Your cousin?! How...?"

"I'm not sure. But it has something to do with alien DNA from my mother."

Of course! That would totally explain his stellar intellectual abilities.

"Welcome aboard," Jesse said." As I nervously entered the craft, I saw a

small nameplate on the hatch door: "Lockheed TR-3B, Astra." I scanned the ceiling for an arrow pointing to the restroom, but there was none. Obvious design flaw.

Jesse inquired, "How have you been — aside from your wrist? Still throbbing?"

"How did you know...?"

He smiled. "They're required, by treaty, to keep complete records of all human encounters — but they would have anyway. You should see the huge computers they use to store millennia of activity!" I imagined a bank of enormous IBM PCs, each with hundreds of floppy disk drives.

"I've read all of your entries."

That made at least four entities spying on me, if you count Santa Claus and God.

His smile turned to a frown, and his eyes became misty, "And I've read the late Daniel Palchek's records, I'm sorry to say. In case you're wondering, it was no lab accident."

It all started to make sense. "Which is why—"

"Why someone who lives by the motto 'All for Our Country' turns into a mutineer."

Jesse a mutineer? Wow.

I changed the subject back to my wrist. "What the hell is it?" I demanded. "What, some sort of control or listening device?"

"Nah, they have no interest in controlling you or listening to you. It's a tag. They tagged you and threw you back, like scientists do with wild animals."

"Why me?"

You invited them, when you contacted them telepathically. "

"I did what?"

"You sent them a message, all those years ago, from your front lawn. Remember 'Show yourself!'?"

The realization hit me like an Air Force-issue pistol: I had done all this to myself! It was my own damn fault! How humiliating! Maybe the Universe (or some benevolent deity) was telling me not to blame others for my personal problems.

Jesse went on to explain the aircraft's technology, which was reminiscent of Professor Palchek's drunken demonstration of the Thomas Townsend Brown Effect. Simply stated (if that's even possible): there's a plasma-filled tube in the center of the crew compartment. The plasma — mercury- and thorium-based — is highly pressurized, heated, and spun (like a Thirsty Cactus plate) to create a super-conductive field. The tube has counter-rotating shafts, which combine to disrupt gravity on any mass within proximity. Sandia and Livermore laboratories developed the technology, which was reverse-engineered from crashed alien craft.

"Spinning mercury?" I responded. "That's basic Vril technology."

"Too close for comfort," Jessie replied.

He continued his show-and-tell, "The vehicle's outer coating is reactive to radar stimulation and is able to change its reflectiveness and color. The polymer skin can make the vehicle look like a small aircraft or a flying cylinder, or even become invisible."

"A Romulan cloaking device?" I exclaimed. "For real?"

He went on to explain that propulsion is provided by thrusters mounted at all three corners of the outer platform.

"The thrusters can operate in the atmosphere using a nuclear reactor. Or in the upper atmosphere using hydrogen-oxygen propulsion. Or in outer space using a combination of both. The original prototype, aka the Alien Reproduction Vehicle, used zero-point energy, like the crashed saucers we recovered.

"Rockwell made the engines," he added. "But the project was developed and fabricated at the Lockheed Skunk Works." To me, it meant that, within the secret Skunk Works, there was a super-secret sub-organization which doesn't just work on spy planes. I felt an entirely inappropriate surge of pride well up in me. The company which had under-appreciated me, fired me, and probably wanted to kill me... was still, irrationally... mine! Hooray for my team!

If the above technical information sounds familiar, it's because it's all been revealed before — but so has a torrent of nonsense, intentionally designed to hide the truth, by burying it under an avalanche of preposterous lies (super-soldiers, time travelers, inter-dimensional beings). It's all basic spy-craft, turned against the public.

Jesse showed me the three-volume TR-3B owner's manual, which went into excruciating detail. I wondered if there was a users' group.

"Like to take a ride?" he offered.

"Would I?!!"

"Choose your destination, anywhere on the planet. I've got a few minutes before my next pick-up."

"Pick-up? What are you, some sort of taxi driver?"

"More like an underground railroad conductor," he said, flashing a broad grin, "helping the enlightened and compromised to escape. Now, let's take the shuttle for a spin."

We did so, literally. The TR-3B revolved slowly as it leapt forward almost instantaneously. In a second, we had risen about 100 feet into the air. I marveled at not feeling any excessive G-forces — in fact, none at all! It was then that I noticed my car being approached by a nondescript motor pool Chevrolet.

"Does this thing have any weapons?" I inquired.

"Weapons?"

"Like phaser cannons or photon torpedoes." I pointed to the MISBs on the viewing scope.

"Not really," Jesse replied. "But I have this." He pressed a button, but nothing seemed to happen.

That was less than spectacular," I complained.

Electromagnetic pulses are silent but deadly," he replied.

"EMPs are SBDs," I noted to myself.

"Wait until they try to start their car or use a two-way radio," Jesse reassured me. "They have a long walk ahead of them."

"I would have preferred an explosion," I grumbled.

Jesse placed a control bowl in his cupped hand. "Where to?"

"The football field at Tina's school, 2137 East Avenue R, Palmdale, CA 93550. And step on it!"

Jesse said something to his cousin that sounded like *"Scrim'bixit Flab'agnizzi."* The grey alien complied by obediently entering the address into some sort of navigation system. Suddenly, Jesse's minoring in linguistics made sense to me.

I added, "And could you please implement the cloaking device? If someone spots us and reports it to MUFON, I might have to investigate myself!"

My own parked TR3B receded in the blink of an eye. As I watched Jesse and his putative cousin pilot the TR-3B, it resolved the trillion-dollar question: ours or theirs? The answer was: both — thanks to what Jesse later explained to me was the Grand Alliance, a treaty with the aliens negotiated by President Eisenhower in 1954, in between his golf games.

Eventually, I had all of my other questions answered, too. Here are the top five bullet points:

- Aliens have been here for tens of thousands of years, sharing the planet with us.
- They administer mining operations and interplanetary trade routes.
- They come in all shapes, sizes, colors, and intentions.
- They have bases underwater, in the Antarctic ice, in volcanos, and on the Moon.

All that talk about how they suddenly became interested in us when we started using nuclear weapons? That never made any sense. If they're millions of miles away — what, we're going to upset some sort of delicate cosmic balance? They're our terrestrial next-door neighbors, and don't want us wrecking the neighborhood! In essence, E.T. is a NIMBY.

And the fifth bullet point:

- In general, the black triangles are ours; the abductions are theirs; and the assassinations are courtesy of the energy conglomerates and the government agencies they control.

Free energy! That was the killer. Literally. To maintain that secret, many have died by "accidents," "suicides," and "unexplained disappearances."

In ancient Roman drama, a play would often end with a god descending from above by means of stage machinery. He would tie up all the loose plot points and make everything whole again. They called it *deus ex machina,* which translates as "God from a machine."

"Jesse, I have a motto for you: *Deus Beatus Ex Machina."* My little quip earned me a chuckle. All those years after Latin class, Jesse understood it meant "God*rich* from a Machine."

I gazed out the view port and saw the football field approaching rapidly, which is an understatement when you're traveling at Mach 12. We landed, and I ran the two blocks to Tina's apartment. She was puzzled to see me at her door, panting like a fugitive from remedial gym class.

"Wade, what are you doing here?"

"Are you ready for your fondest wish to be granted?" I blurted out.

"What on earth?!"

"I have something amazing to show you! We need to hurry," I pleaded.

We sprinted back to the football field. When Tina gazed upon my fancy new conveyance, which took up most of the gridiron, she was overwhelmed! I smiled, and smugly inquired, "Is this close enough for you?"

All she could say was, "Now this is more your style!" Moral: Never think for a moment that women aren't impressed by what you drive.

I climbed the ramp to the open hatch and extended my hand. "Care to join me?" I bravely ventured.

"Zabotny," she replied, while tentatively touching the hatch door to make sure it was real. "Zabotny!"

Epilogue

My guess is that it's now about 2002, Earth time. I've spent years writing this account... let us say... somewhere else (sorry, I can't reveal where for security reasons). Since you're reading this, it means that Tina's brother Merrill was able to get the manuscript published. If you want the truth about our secret space program, the alien presence, and zero-point energy to be revealed, please pass this on to your friends and family. The more people who know, the safer we will all be — maybe even safe enough for us to return home someday — although I'm not even sure why we would want to.

After all these years, it's satisfying to have won my UFO debate with Jesse — although our chess record is currently 374-to-zero, in favor of you-know-*whom*. One of these days I'm going to beat that jug-headed son-of-an-alien!

Before we left Earth, I managed to acquire all seventy-one of P. G. Wodehouse's novels, and I reread them regularly. It connects me with my childhood home and more innocent times.

Tina and I are very happy here, living among the thousands of mutineers, fellow escapees, and other off-planet assets (mostly Earthlings). We've created quite a mini-civilization, with Jesse as benevolent dictator, Elsa Zabotny as Chief of Security, and Tina as school superintendent. Our daughter, Astra — without the benefit of any alien DNA at all — is the brightest student in our colony's scholastic firmament. You could say that she's this world's Star Pupil.

And you should see the way she pilots that TR-3B!

THREE POEMS

Glen Armstrong

From the Center of an X

We are a people of eyes
and other dots,

glass beads and tiny circles
cut from the center

of an x. They never
welcomed us properly,

never had us
over for tea and awkward

conversation,
never got us to stop

trembling. Our ancestors
understood crosshairs

before scopes even existed,
the dangers in the gauzy space

they occupied.
They told stories equally

loved by haters and Haitians
who want their fight song back.

Some of the confetti thrown
in his honor finds its way

into the f-holes
of Charles's upright bass.

Glen Armstrong

From Her Veranda

She ventures from her veranda
and shouts,

"There is nothing but cold air
at the beginning

of that which matters,
The Rugby World Cup or a love

affair, for example."
She stirs a little something in me

that needed stirring.
It's early in the morning,

and the January nights,
though shrinking, are still too long.

There's too much to remember
and not enough spin on the ball.

(There is no ball.)
There are too many horses

and not enough warm clothing
to go around.

There are too many sheer bathrobes
and not enough

taxi cabs for those wishing
to depart.

Return to Redondo Beach

To go swimming is to go to sea with no boat
and very little ambition. I return a little
sunburned with no stories of my adventures
in strange and distant lands. In ancient
times, teenagers would dance on the beach
to a network of transistor radios all tuned
to the same station, but now the young folks
stay home to post pictures of their bodies
on the internet: dancing, eating enormous
amounts of cheese, making love, vomiting
the cheese, getting dressed, applying makeup,
casting spells in the park ... All the stars
have disappeared, and cloud cover has made
the night sky bright but unclear. I take
the moon's fullness on faith, its shape
obscured but its light still strong enough
for me to read the flier for a punk rock
concert someone left on my car while I
was swimming.

TWO POEMS

E.L. Douglas

Cardinals

The steps to the front porch grow steeper every year.
The paint on the rocking chairs have long since chipped.
But I still sit there, gazing at the silver stars.

I brew cinnamon tea — your favorite.
There used to be more cups on the shelves,
but now I just need one.
I bring the tea out to the garden,
and the box with a loose hinge.

A cardinal lands in front of me,
on the angel statue forever watching
over our porch.

Every day, sunrise to sunset,
I rifle through hundreds of postcards,
all taken from spinning racks from
every date over fifty years,
piled into this perfect box.

Picnics against avocado and kumquat trees,
forever captioned, *Wish you were here.*

Greetings from Pigeon Forge,
first degree burns from
a clumsy cooking class.

Fishing on Lake Erie,
a beautiful day frozen in time
on a four-by-six card.

Our old address is on the back.
A forever stamp.

But you're still here.

You're in the garden.
You're in your workshop.
You're in the postcards.

The cardinal flies away.

E.L. Douglas

Yellow

Neon signs flicker and flash.
Pothole puddles are a sickly reflection
of synthetic sunlight.

The sun has long since set.
The shadow of the moon casts no light and
I rely on the signs of the late night diners.

Golden arches,
Butter over waffles,
Overhead lights that look like egg yolks.

I walk alone through the city of steel.
My raincoat prevents me from
becoming one of the city's shadows.

I count the streetlamps that
wash me in a circle of yellow light.
I subtract the bulbs that have burned out.

In the darkness, I make out
scrawled handwriting over the bookstore sign:
PERMANENTLY CLOSED.

The yellow marker runs in the rain.

I tug my hood further over my head.

I try to disappear into the darkness,
like the city had years ago.

My faded golden key struggles in the lock.
I toss off my yellow raincoat.
The amber lights barely turn on.

My eyes are drawn to an unusual spot of color.
In the corner of the living room is
a lemon tree.

I dig my nails into one of the yellow fruits,
letting the juice run over my hand.
It's real. It's life.

The Go Rub Yourself Sonnets

Jack Granath

I

We met while stuck inside a muddy hole
Some twilit bar had flushed us halfway through.
Hannah put one hand against my soul,
Let down her hair, and shoved me up the flue.

The wet earth fit me like a falcon's hood.
I couldn't breathe but didn't really care—
The dying I was doing felt damn good,
My body swaddled in her bread-warm hair.

A shudder then, that terrible cliché,
Sufficed me and I landed in the street,
Contented, briefly hog-like where I lay,
Sprawled in a slush of blood at Hanna's feet.

The evening ended with a goodnight kiss,
The kind that feels, at bottom, bottomless.

Jack Granath

I I

I inched awake, my eyes sealed shut with slaver,
A dozen mastiffs tearing at the bed,
Panting after any petty favor
That might be yawningly distributed.

Hannah told me they were only friends,
And I believed her, even when they bit.
I argued, calculating dividends,
Let's melt together and be done with it,

And she agreed, if evanescently.
She shambled bravely through the ritual
By stepping over Butch to stand with me,
While Rufus plainted something pitiful.

I didn't realize it was a game
Until their laughter tipped its hand and came.

III

But no game can compete with one on one,
Which Hannah called for after our debauch.
She guaranteed me steaming loads of fun
And crouched down like a chimpanzee to watch.

My adversary was a chewing goon,
Who chose a rapier and a piece of meat
As weapons for a lazy afternoon
Of mulching me beneath his filthy feet.

I faced him with a page of day-old talk
That stropped the rusty razor of my mind
Until it flattered forth a tomahawk
And left my Western history behind.

I struggled fiercely, foaming, wolf-dance-hearted,
Slipped, got up, and then the battle started.

Jack Granath

IV

And from the far end of the sewer pipe,
Emerging on a devastated plain,
Two figures of apocalyptic type
Crawled across the shadows like a stain.

One of them was called the Comely Man.
The other, somewhat uglier, was me,
Meditating on my master plan
To live and let all interlopers be

Consumed by fire. We had to talk about her,
He with a playboy's crooked, shrugging smile,
I, the ardor-hardened double doubter,
Between clenched teeth while disemboguing bile.

Trust is like corn, a thing to sow and reap.
I think he tried to kill me in my sleep.

V

Maybe she found the damaged part attractive
Or pitied it and tingled as she did,
Her motherstuff benignly hyperactive—
Kiss of cow and eightfold hug of squid.

I didn't mind. I took what I could get
And let her salve my spiritual ache.
I played with probabilities and bet
My pleasures on a bountiful mistake.

My math was lacking, but I beat the odds
Until the two-by-four I wielded broke
And I lay cursing her by all the gods
Of my imagination, and she spoke,

Not having heard one red-hot word I said.
She dropped her jeans. I dropped and quieted.

VI

There followed five wet weeks of oily joy,
A beach scene in a movie with guitars,
And then she licked to life another boy
And jilted me beneath a scum of stars.

But in those weeks we gorged on love like leeches
Plastered to the ankle of a slut,
Sucked blood until we blew our farthest reaches
By reaching for a door forever shut.

The future lay behind it, and the past,
And all the other parasites of touch,
Those mewling lies, that pullulating caste
Of promises that lick their teeth too much.

Time's hooligans exulted, being free,
Then thrashed me with my own philosophy.

VII

My head exploded, it was no big deal.
I set off for the party after all
With my pet monkey and my glockenspiel
And an adolescent plan to have a ball.

It felt as if a can of sperm had spilled.
Everyone who's everyone was there,
Including Hannah and the man she killed,
Tangled like a sparrow in her hair.

I took up my position at the bar
And watched that thickset evening drip like wax,
While Hannah worked her magic from afar,
Causing little cocktail heart attacks.

At twelve o'clock I tucked my wound away,
Shouted for silence, and began to play.

Want more great things to read?
Then make sure to get a subscription to *Night Picnic!*

Subscriptions are $35 per year ($45 for libraries) and include three issues. For subscribers outside the US, please add $10. Send checks or money orders to:
Night Picnic Press LLC
P.O. Box 3819
New York, NY 10163-3819

If you'd like to support the publication of the journal, we are grateful for donations of any amount.

Made in the USA
Middletown, DE
20 March 2024